GOLD ENVY

RENA WINTERS

Copyright (C) 2021 Rena Winters

Layout design and Copyright (C) 2021 by Next Chapter

Published 2021 by Next Chapter

Edited by Tyler Colins

Cover art by CoverMint

Mass Market Paperback Edition

This book is a work of fiction. Names, characters, places, and incidents are the product of the author's imagination or are used fictitiously. Any resemblance to actual events, locales, or persons, living or dead, is purely coincidental.

All rights reserved. No part of this book may be reproduced or transmitted in any form or by any means, electronic or mechanical, including photocopying, recording, or by any information storage and retrieval system, without the author's permission.

LADURA -
The World's Greatest Treasure

"La Dura is of the buried past yet it remains
the hope of men and women searching today
and making plans to search tomorrow."

OLD SPANISH PROVERB

PROLOGUE

THERE WERE SOME WHO CAME TO LA DURA, OR TO
where they thought La Dura should be, with copies
of the Jesuit maps and codes ... they failed.

Many others came with different maps, different
codes, or with nothing at all except the fever for gold
and treasure ... they too failed.

Records have been kept since the forties and we
know that each year at least three-thousand Ameri-
cans cross the border in search of La Dura, and that
fifteen hundred never return.

The brutal terrain, Indians, bandits, the drug car-
tels, illness, murder, and the inability to live off the
land ... endless dead-ends ... false trails ... just a few
of the reasons for failure.

The famous and the infamous have searched for
La Dura. The lucky ones are those who returned to
the border empty-handed. The others ... well, their
stories are lost forever, bleaching with their bones
under the warm Mexican sun in some unchartered
canyon.

There are many who believe the gold will never
be found and that the iron door that guards the treasure house of La Dura has been buried, far beyond

the reach of any metal detector, by earthquakes of past centuries.

There is the story that the Apaches have told since La Dura became a dream. It is said that somewhere there is a gold chain and on that chain hangs a Medallion that was made from the gold of La Dura. It shows a beautiful dove trying to rise in flight to escape a striking rattlesnake. Could the legend be true? Could this Medallion be the key to the world's greatest known treasure?

Is the Medallion, if truly there ever was a Medallion, somewhere with the bones of the padres, who were massacred during the great Indian revolt, or did it ever really exist?

There is a story told around campfires on both sides of the border of a Medallion, coated with dust, that hung forgotten in a pawnshop window in Magdalene. Could it be? The tales are endless and varied, but the one told most often is the story of an old Spanish family who knows where the Medallion is hidden and they have ...

Ah, a thousand pardons, *Señor*. You know that so much is legend. Just for a moment, let us suppose this story is fact.

We know that the padres were stealing from the King of Spain. Their ancient records show that they had an underground treasure house where tons of gold bars were stored, to be used for the power and glory of their order. Those records do not lie.

We do know that these Jesuits invented codes that even today we are unable to decipher, and yet, if one had the Medallion and could locate a true copy of the padre's maps ...

There was a rumor, a tale told in whispers, a story that exists without hard facts ... one that I first heard in a little cantina somewhere south of

Sahuaipa. A strange story, about a woman and four men who had somehow obtained the lost Medallion and an ancient map; the details are hazy at best. It seems they went into the mountains, and there the trail ended.

Somewhere in old Mexico, high in the trackless Sierra Madre, far beyond the reach of all known high-tech equipment, the greatest treasure of all awaits discovery.

Who really knows? The legend, it must be a dream, yet I hear it. I have heard it many times before. In the hush before the dawn, at high noon when the desert is hot and still, or when fever racks my body and sweat drenches me like summer rain.

It comes at sunset ... very soft. Like the faint echo of a long-forgotten mission bell. It comes on the wind from the mountains and whispers to me as it plays through the mesquite and chaparral. "Come, come to La Dura ... come to the gold of La Dura."

You see, something deep inside tells me it is not a dream.

It can't be a dream.

Ah, but who really knows, *Señor*?
Maybe, you will find La Dura.
Or maybe, it will be me.

CHAPTER ONE

1987

IN THIS REMOTE PLACE, THE MIST OF EARLY MORNING was slow to rise, hiding for a time behind the distant mountains. On three sides, the thick growth of mesquite was creeping in on the clearing that once housed a small Catholic mission. In the background, bougainvillea spilled over crumbling adobe walls. Two saddled horses were tied to the one remaining door of the old mission. The horse's breath made small clouds of vapor in the cold morning air.

Hot coals held a battered coffee pot. A man squatted beside the coals, smoking a thin cigar and taking frequent sips from the tin cup that held the steaming liquid. A black, low-crowned hat the Mexicans call a *tejano* put his face in shadow. He wore a black jacket that was showing age and a great deal of dust from desert riding. A clean white shirt was tucked into faded jeans that tapered down hard legs into worn, handcrafted boots. Around his waist was a gun belt and on his right hip hung a .45-caliber Colt with a well-oiled grip.

He changed his position and tilted his hat so that the feeble rays of the sun could touch his face. In his veins ran the blood of Spanish Dons. His hawk-like nose, clear brown eyes, and olive complexion complimented his even white teeth. Underneath the band of the hat, the black hair was shot with gray. The deep lines in his face contrasted his well- muscled body.

His name was Francisco Ropero. A Renaissance man whose family emigrated from Spain some two-hundred years before and built a cattle empire in what was now southern Arizona. Although he was taught the cattle business by his grandfather and father, and was attentive to their teachings, his heart and mind were filled with thoughts of high adventure and stories of treasure to be had for the taking. Now, danger and possible death were tracking his every move, and the border and safety were a long twelve hours away.

Flipping the butt of his cigar into the coals, he called in a soft voice, "*Niño*, wake up!"

Near, where the horses were tied, was a small body wrapped in a blanket.

Suddenly, the head of a young Mexican boy popped up. "Forgive me, *Señor*. How did I sleep so long?"

Ropero laughed softly. "When one is young, one can sleep, the sleep of the saints. Come, have some coffee and biscuits."

The boy scrambled out of his blanket, rolled it up, and came to the campfire. He was dressed in a loose-fitting Mexican wedding shirt, faded jeans, and dark brown boots. In his face was a blend of the Indians who once ruled this land, mixed with the bloodlines of some long forgotten Conquistador. "If my father knew I was spending my life sleeping, he would never let me go with you again."

The boy dug into the sack of biscuits as Ropero poured coffee into an extra tin cup.

"Jesus, I promise not to tell if you won't."

Taking the cup from Ropero, he squatted by the fire, biting into his biscuit.

Ropero seemed thoughtful. His eyes were troubled and he measured each word slowly as he spoke. Jesus stopped eating and listened carefully.

"Jesus, you are still a boy, a boy of only eleven years, but I am going to give you the responsibility of a man."

Reaching inside his shirt pocket, Ropero pulled out a gold chain. Attached to the chain was what appeared to be a locket or a medallion. It flashed in the sunlight as Ropero cupped it in his hands and showed it to Jesus.

"This is the Medallion of the lost La Dura. As you have heard in story and song, this is the key to the greatest known treasure in the entire world."

Jesus' eyes were dazzled by the Medallion sparkling in the sun. Carved in the gold was a beautiful dove, rising on the wing to escape the deadly fangs of a striking rattlesnake. The boy felt a shiver go up his spine as Ropero continued.

"I don't know why, because I have found no evidence, but I think we're being followed. If this is true, the reason is the Medallion and this envelope."

From the inner pocket of his jacket he took out a sealed envelope made of heavy parchment. "Your father has been at our ranch since the day he was born. We grew up together. Your grandfather helped my grandfather drive cattle from Texas to stock our ranch back in pioneer days. The lives of our families are intertwined forever, *amigo*. That is why I am putting this in your care."

The boy was wide-eyed, shaking his head. He didn't want to hear this kind of talk. "Oh *Señor*, do not speak of possible trouble. We are only one day away from the border. The time of great adventures is past history. We are in a modern world."

"Jesus, listen to me and listen well. It could be the year five thousand but in this part of Mexico, time has stood still. The clocks stopped somewhere back in the 16th century. Remember the little mission where I left you while I went to the mountains? Nothing had changed. It would have been the same in the time of Cortez. The old Padre is living the same way other padres did centuries ago. Trust me, Jesus, the old fears, the legends, and the lost La Dura are real ... *very* real."

Jesus shook his head, not wanting to believe what he was hearing, but Ropero pressed on.

"My intuition tells me something is wrong, I know it. Now, here is what you're to do, and no questions, *comprende*?" He placed the chain with the Medallion over the head and around the neck of the boy, Ropero then handed him the parchment envelope containing the map.

If anything happens to me, or if I tell you, you're to ride for the border as hard and as fast as possible. Don't hesitate and don't look back. Put the Medallion away until my daughter is grown, then give it to her. It will be my legacy. The best thing I could ever leave her."

Jesus buttoned his shirt to hide the Medallion.

"*Momento, patron,* your daughter is only a month old. What would she know of La Dura?"

A smile played at the corner of Ropero's mouth as the memory of his infant daughter flashed through his mind. "That is now, Jesus. Someday she will be a woman, a beautiful woman, and the ranch, the cattle, and La Dura will be hers."

Rising, they threw the remains of their coffee on the coals and Jesus kicked dirt on the fire, then put the map in his saddlebag. Ropero went to his horse and put the empty coffee pot, sack of biscuits, and the cups into his bedroll and cinched it tight behind his saddle.

"This is why it is so important that you make the border should we have trouble. If I don't make it, you will be there to guide her in the years when she needs help. As you know, her mother died giving her life, so she has only you and I to lean on … and at least one of us must be there."

A reflective mood came over him and for a few seconds, he rubbed his horse's ear. "This evening we'll cross the desert and be home."

He vaulted into the saddle and a few seconds later Jesus mounted his horse and they headed north toward the border.

CHAPTER TWO

THE COUNTRY WAS RUGGED. DEEP CANYONS, NARROW trails and a great deal of undergrowth made the going slow. By mid-day, sweat drenched the faces of the riders. Breaking through the trees, they rode down an incline ending at a rippling stream.

They dismounted and led their horses where they could drink while standing in the deep shade of old trees that lined the bank. Both Ropero and Jesus got their fill of the cold, clear water and munched on biscuits Ropero had pulled from the sack in his bedroll. Wiping his face on his coat sleeve, he pointed to a canyon opening fifty yards on the far side of the stream.

"If there is to be trouble, it will happen here. The canyon up ahead has walls so narrow that you can almost reach out and touch the sides as you ride through. It runs for about two miles. But once we break out on the far side, we'll come down onto the desert and the ride to the border should be easy."

"Maybe we can ride to Sahuaipa and rent a Jeep and drive to the border?"

Ropero laughed at the thought. They filled their canteens and made sure the saddles were cinched tight. No breeze moved the leaves and one had to strain to hear the soft murmur of the stream. It was as if the whole world were watching and waiting— waiting for *something* to happen.

Slowly, they mounted their horses and moved through the stream, stopping a few feet from the mouth of the canyon, whose towering walls seemed to reach to the sky.

"Here's the way we'll handle this. We're going to ride like hell through this place. You go first and I'll follow. Just remember that if anything should happen, don't come back. Don't even look back. Just ride as hard and as fast as you can until you cross the border. *Vaya con dios.*"

CHAPTER THREE

JESUS SLAPPED HIS MOUNT AND HASTENED AWAY AT A gallop. Ropero waited, maybe five seconds, and then drove his horse forward. At full speed, they hit the narrow canyon, whose towering walls nearly blotted out the sun. They were halfway through when a rifle shot rang out.

Ropero's horse stumbled and went down. Throwing himself clear, he rolled and came up with the big Colt in his hand. He saw Jesus stop and turn back as another shot ricocheted off the canyon wall. "

"Ride, Jesus, ride!"

A rifle bullet kicked up sand and rock at the feet of Jesus' horse. It panicked and reared, but Jesus got it under control, turned, and raced through the canyon toward the border.

As Ropero watched, Jesus vanished. A bullet ripped through his left shoulder, spinning him around. He dove into the underbrush. Blood was seeping from the wound. He scrambled to his knees as a hail of bullets hit the trees and rocks where he had been standing. Pushing to his feet, he was racing

for cover when a greasy gunman stepped from behind a tree.

"Far enough, señor!"

Like a well-oiled machine, the Colt leveled in
Ropero's hand and his bullet tore open the gunman's
throat; blood spurted from a gaping wound. The rifle
dropped from his fingers and the light of life died in
his eyes as he pitched forward.

Ropero sprinted for the other side of the trail as
he heard the feet of runners and horses crashing
through the bushes and undergrowth. As he dove behind a rock, a bullet entered his leg and he rolled beyond his intended cover.

Two gunmen stepped into the clearing. One
smiled as he raised his rifle. Ropero made the grin
permanent as he shot him between the eyes, and
then pumped two shots into his friend. Ropero
looked at his bloody thigh and started crawling toward higher cover when he saw a man on horseback
about to break through the bushes.

The Colt whipped into firing position, but before
he could squeeze the shot off, a man materialized behind him, swinging his rifle like a club. It caught
Ropero on the side of his head. His sight was shattered into a million fragments.

He managed to make out the dim shape of a
rider who had dismounted and was coming toward
him. He tried to raise his gun hand, but the dim
shape kicked the gun away.

Before he sank into a deep black hole, Ropero
realized that this man was wearing silver-buckled leg-
gings of soft leather with fancy silver spurs. The man
was busy grinding one of those spurs into Ropero's
empty gun hand, causing his blood to make wild de-
signs as it ran off his fingertips.

CHAPTER FOUR

A WHITE LIGHT SEARED ROPERO'S EYEBALLS AND ATE into his brain. The whole world was swirling and whirling, and nothing stood still. From somewhere Ropero heard a voice.

"All right, *bastardo*, tell us where the map and the Medallion of La Dura are hidden."

Ropero was aware of shooting pains in various parts of his body. He was on the ground, stripped to the waist, and his face and hair were covered with dry sand. In the background, someone was ripping his jacket and shirt to shreds.

Rough hands grabbed him and jerked him to his feet. The man who had slammed him in the head with the rifle threw what was left of his jacket and shirt at the feet of the man wearing the silver spurs.

"There's nothing in the jacket. Tell me where in the hell could it be?"

Another dirty rider with wild, unkempt hair joined the group. "Maybe we should chase the kid. Maybe he's got it. We can sure as hell catch that little Indio before he reaches the border. We have fresh horses and ..."

Ropero heard what they said about catching the

kid and struggled with the men holding him, but Silver Spurs paid no attention.

He flecked a speck of dust from his black jacket and smiled a cruel smile as he interrupted the dirty rider. "Don't be a fool. He wouldn't trust a treasure or a map to an Indio. If you remember, when we crucified and burned the Padre on his church door, he was screaming that Ropero had the map and the Medallion when he left the Mission. Since they are not with him, it means he buried them before he rode into the canyon. It may take a while, but he's going to tell us the location. Strip him naked and bring him over here. I have lots of time to wait for him to talk."

Ropero was jerked forward and his shoulder wound started to bleed profusely. Although he struggled, the men pulled off his boots and stripped his faded jeans from his white body. Placing stakes in the ground, he was tied spread-eagle.

The leader walked over to view his men's work. His body blocked out the brutal rays of the sun.

Ropero opened his eyes to look into the pale, narrow face with slightly slanted hooded eyes. This man was a *gringo*. His black eyes seemed to bore into Ropero's very soul as the thin lips moved to speak. "Do you want to die slow or fast?"

The question hung in the air as the man with the silver spurs looked at Ropero's body. Blood was still tricking down his shoulder into the mat of hair that covered his chest. The right thigh had a deep tear where a hollow-point bullet had found its mark. The lips of the wound were already turning blue. His body was covered with sweat and rivulets ran from his flat belly into his groin. His genitals were already starting to burn and the right hand where the spur has punctured it was turning a deep red and purple.

"I ask you, *bastardo*, do you want to die slow or fast?"

Ropero looked deep into the coal black eyes. "I don't have the Medallion or the map, so do what you have to do."

Silver Spurs drew a long, slender knife from under his jacket. "You will be happy to tell me everything before you and I are through."

He knelt and with his knife made long shallow slashes down Ropero's body from shoulders to thighs; they became small rivers of blood. He started to rise, then knelt, and carefully slashed an 'X' in Ropero's pubic hair.

"Lorenzo, bring our little friends."

The big Mexican had an ant hill cupped in his hands that he gingerly placed on Ropero's pubis. On the second trip, he forced another ant hill under Ropero's buttocks.

In a few moments, the ants were everywhere in the blood-sweetened crevices of his body. Racing over his genitals, across his eyes, and working their way into his mouth and nostrils.

Silver Spurs stood and walked to Ropero's feet. A cruel smile played across his thin face.

"I'm going to have a nice cold drink. *Salude, amigo.*"

Silver Spurs drank deep from his canteen. Little trickles of clear water made streaks on his dust-covered face. Capping the canteen, he looked down at his captive. "It is cold and very good ... cold and clear and *good*. You, my friend, can have a drink before you die—as soon as you tell me about La Dura."

Ropero's eyes and mouth were crawling with ants. They were everywhere on his body. He was twisting in pain as much as the bonds would allow and he forced the words through his swollen, ant-filled lips, "Damn you to hell!" He bucked his body against the ropes and screamed. "Damn you to hell!"

Silver Spurs picked up a long stick and, with quick movement, slashed it through Ropero's spread legs catching his genitals, and bringing a moan of pain.

"Ah *señor*, you will never know the intimate parts of a woman again. Think about that when you talk of hell. It is you, not I, who is on the way to hell. Unless you talk fast, hell may be a long time coming."

Silver Spurs tired of the game and joined his men in the shade of the trees, where they ate jerky and biscuits washed down by mescal. After eating, some of the men played cards, and some napped while others cleaned their weapons.

As the daylight faded, the mosquitoes joined the ants foraging Ropero's body. At times he screamed for water, but the ants in his throat turned the words into crazy sounds.

Before it was dark, Silver Spurs visited his captive. Looking down he saw the ravages the ants had made. Ropero's genitals and legs were burned bright red by the sun and covered with bites. His lips and face were swollen and ravaged.

"Well, *señor*, shall we talk of La Dura? My men can drown the ants, and then you can tell me where you left the Medallion and the map. After we check that out, I'll let you die. It will be quick and your pain will be over."

With superhuman strength, Ropero forced his head up, and despite the ants that foraged through his mouth, he screamed, "Fuck you! You will never have La Dura.",

Silver Spurs responded with a chilling smile.

"We shall see, my friend … come morning, we shall see."

CHAPTER FIVE

THE DESERT TURNED COLD. THE SCREAMS AND sounds of agony from the prisoner made the hours seem endless and the men did not sleep well. At breakfast, even Silver Spurs had dark smudges under his eyes, showing the strain of waiting for their prisoner to break.

Lorenzo expressed the thoughts of all the men. "This time has been wasted. He will die before the day is over and we won't know any more about La Dura than we did before."

Silver Spurs snarled. "He has hidden the Medallion and the map. Remember the last moments at the mission—when the Padre was nailed to the door and the fire was burning the flesh from his body? In between screaming his prayers for mercy, he told us that Ropero had both the Medallion and the map. That, and a Hail Mary was the last thing to come from his bubbling lips.

I have no doubt that before his soul departed, the good priest told the truth. I intend to get both the map and the Medallion today. Lorenzo, when you finish eating, make up some sweet water from the sugar sack."

He walked to where Ropero was staked out. The sun was already broiling hot and it was only mid-morning. The body was burned to a purple hue. Where the skin had never been exposed to the sun's rays it had cracked and the ants had slowly torn the flesh away in the creases that were cut by Silver Spur's knife. The man's genitals were burned, swollen and dripping. Where the face should be a giant hill of ants was going in and out of the open hole that passed for a mouth and clogged the opening of the nostrils. The raw throat kept trying to form the word "water."

"Wa ... ta, wa ... ta, plea ... ease God, give me ... wa ... ta."

"I'm going to give you water and you're going to see the sun, and then you will tell me where the Medallion and the map are hidden. Lorenzo, bring the sweet water!"

The men gathered around as Lorenzo brought the sugared water he had mixed in a canteen.

"Good, now get some more of our friends and we will take care of the business at hand."

With care, Silver Spurs poured the sugared water making sure there was a heavy concentration of the sticky stuff over the genitals, mouth, nose, and eyes.

Ropero made sucking noises trying to taste the water, but his mouth and tongue had been destroyed. Lorenzo and another gunman came back with fresh ant hills. Again, they were placed on Ropero's pubis and under his buttocks. The ants tasting the sweet water went wild.

Crossing to Ropero's head, Silver Spurs took first one eyelid, then the other, and slashed them with his knife so that his captive was unable to keep either the sun or the crazed ants out of his eyes. One of Silver Spurs crew had captured a scorpion and pushed it into the tangle of hair in Ropero's right armpit.

The men roared with laughter as the scorpion struck Ropero's sweat-drenched flesh with its powerful stinger tail. This brought new screams from the tortured man who was on the verge of losing his mind.

"Wa ... ta! Wa ... ta!"

Silver Spurs knelt by his head. "Maybe there will be water in hell for you, or you can have water now. Cold, cold water. Tell me, where is the Medallion and the map of La Dura?"

For one lucid moment, Ropero was able to focus on what had happened. Sensing this, Silver

Spurs indicated that one of his men keep the ants out of his eyes and to brush them from his mouth.

A strange gurgle that might pass for laughter came from Ropero's ant-eaten throat. He tried to form words with his tortured lips.

"Put some water on his face and mouth. He's going to tell us about La Dura."

One of the men opened his canteen and let clear, cold water gush over Ropero's face, washing away the ants.

"La Dura." He tried to form words. " Me ... dal ... lion ... gone. B ... bo ... boy to ... ook ... them. Sa ... safe now ... ahhhhhhh."

The toe of Silver Spur's boot smashed into Ropero's side, breaking some ribs. "You *bastardo*, you tricked us. You sent everything ahead with that stupid Indio boy. Damn you. Damn your soul to hell."

His hand closed on the butt of his .357 Magnum and it cleared leather. His lips curled back over his teeth as he raised it to fire. Then the rage passed, and slowly he returned the pistol to his holster.

"Lorenzo, bring my horse, we are going to leave this cursed place."

Slowly, he walked to where his body blocked out the sun and Ropero, who had only seconds before the ants returned to eat his eyes, could see him.

"You win my friend. I am going to let you live."

Silver Spurs looked up into the blue sky, where several vultures were circling. "Yes, I'm going to let you live so that the vultures can come down and rip what is left of your eyes out. They will drive their beaks into your burned body and eat your flesh. I want you to know every step on the road to hell."

Lorenzo delivered a beautiful black horse and Silver Spurs swung into the saddle. He leaned forward and lowered his voice as if to tell Ropero a secret.

"In another lifetime, others will seek La Dura, but La Dura is a legend that is written in blood. He who finds La Dura will pay with his life."

Tall in the saddle he touched the brim of his Stetson, "*Adiós, amigo.*" Wheeling his horse, he galloped away with his men in pursuit. The time was high noon.

Ropero forced himself high enough to watch the departing riders. A gasp issued from his ant-filled mouth and his head dropped back. He felt a vulture's claws sink into the flesh of his upper thigh and white hot pain surged through his body as the roughness of the beak probed his burned, ant-eaten genitals. A silent scream filled his throat as his lid-less eyes were covered by the shadow of giant wings.

———

Death did not come easy this sweltering day. Had it been recorded, Francisco Juan Ropero departed this life at 2:37 P.M., somewhere in Sonora, Mexico.

CHAPTER SIX

Twenty-Seven Years Later

The sun beat down on the Amtrak station where the tower clock read 3:30 P.M. The few people on the loading platform threw quick glances up the track and consulted wristwatches, while others stayed in the shade and watched the workers at the corral and feeding pens by the spur track that ran a few yards away.

Soon to depart were arriving passengers. Many were making last minute calls on cell phones. Drivers found parking places and their charges hurried into the station with a variety of luggage. People coming to greet travelers filled the platform and the hum of voices was everywhere. The train was only a speck in the distance when the sun struck it, flaring brilliantly for a moment, as it roared toward its destination.

Cab drivers who had been napping came to life, and the bulk of the people who had remained in the air-conditioned shelter of the station lobby moved onto the platform as the train took shape through the dust of the desert.

The silver shell quivered to a stop. A conductor

stepped down and the passengers started their exit as the waiting crowd surged forward.

First off was a man in his fifties. An executive in expensive Western clothes. A plump, pretty woman and four children surrounded him, laughing, as they headed toward an SUV where a small dog stood in a partially closed window barking a welcome.

A woman with a baby was greeted by in-laws. A young man, whose pale skin confirmed he was not from the Southwest, was met by an older couple whose weathered faces spoke of long hours spent in the desert.

The beautiful, expensively dressed woman exiting the train was Maria Ropero, last of a proud Spanish family, the sole owner of a giant cattle empire along the Arizona/Mexican border. Her mother had died in childbirth and for twenty-seven years, her father's fate was never known. It was presumed that he died at the hands of outlaws somewhere in Mexico.

She was tall with shoulder-length dark hair; fine breasts thrust upward, and long slender legs. The sensuous aroma of her delicate perfume mixed with the smells of the train, its passengers, the cattle in the feeding pens, and the desert. Her flashing, dark brown eyes searched for someone. Then she saw him and a beautiful smile of even white teeth framed by warm red lips appeared.

"Jesus, Jesus ... over here!"

A good-looking, dark-skinned man with sparkling eyes shouldered his way through the crowd. Now thirty-eight years of age, Jesus had grown tall and slim in the years since his ride with Maria's father on his final journey. A gentle smile lit his face as he made his way to her side.

"Ms. Maria. Good to see you. The sun just doesn't shine as bright when you're gone."

A veil of weariness mixed with deep concern slipped over Maria's lovely features. "Jesus, you have been flattering me since I was a little girl, but I love it. Let's start for the ranch, I feel very tired."

They worked their way through the crowd and located the four-wheel drive that bore the ranch crest. Jesus put Maria's bags in the back as she entered the passenger side. He slid under the wheel and with a roar of power, the car moved forward into the mainstream of modern day Tucson, then out toward the desert and the rolling hills beyond.

They had left the city far behind before Maria spoke, the words rushing out as though a dam within had broken. "My trip was a failure. With the foreign situation, oil, industry, and agriculture in such a state of flux, the bankers have no interest in talking about the amount of money we need to survive. They don't understand and they don't care about the years of drought or the thousands of cattle we have lost. Of course, if I would give them the land to build fancy condos and resorts, that is a whole different story. I will never sell them our land."

Jesus reached out his hand to cover hers and spoke in a quiet voice.

"Something will happen. I know. Everyone at the ranch knows you did your very best."

Maria let her head drop back against the seat. "My best was not good enough. In six months, we have payments to make that are impossible. If we can't get a loan, and I mean a large loan, we're going to lose the ranch. I don't know where to turn. I don't know what to do."

"What about Randolph? After all, he's your attorney and a powerful man in his own right. His whole world is putting investment and financial packages together. Hasn't he been able to help?"

Maria looked deeply into Jesus eyes. "Jesus, the people I met with back east, Randolph sent me to them. He said they would listen, that they would be willing to make the loan, but there was nothing."

The dust swirled behind them as they went deeper into the desert. Something was troubling Jesus.

Then, with great reluctance, he said, "I had hoped with all my heart that I would never have to discuss this with you, but now I must. I can't let you lose everything. You see Maria, your father had a secret, and I am the only one who knows what that secret is. He trusted me with it."

Maria started to say something, then looked away. She paused for several seconds as the desert rolled by, then turned to Jesus and spoke softly. "If my father had a secret, I think it's time that I know what it is, although how it can have any bearing on the situation with the ranch, I have no idea."

"This evening, I will tell you."

They were moving faster now as the clouds of dust behind them grew bigger. They passed through an open gate and started the climb toward the top of the hill, where a large Spanish-style ranch house overlooked thousands of acres spread out below.

CHAPTER SEVEN

THE ORANGE SUN WAS LOW IN THE WESTERN SKY AS Maria and Jesus leaned back in their chairs at the table on the veranda of the big ranch house. The empty glasses, a half-filled pitcher of iced tea, and plate of cookies had been pushed to one side. In front of Maria was the parchment map and the gold Medallion of La Dura.

"That's the story, Maria, the whole story. Your father told me to ride as hard as I could for the border and I never saw him again."

Maria held the Medallion up for a closer look. A dove was starting to soar toward the sun while below a rattlesnake was striking, trying to kill the dove before it could fly to safety. "It is so beautiful and, yet, I feel a chill running through me."

A frown clouded Jesus' handsome face. "My people say that La Dura is cursed, that the gold is covered with blood, yet there are many who would sell their souls to find the treasure."

Tenderly, Maria placed the Medallion on the map. "I have heard the legends of your people since I was a little girl. Most of them are just that, legends, stories to make life around a campfire less lonely."

Determination masked her beautiful face. "Maybe this is an omen. Without money, we will lose the ranch. Maybe this is why my father died. What we need are a couple of men, men who know Mexico, men who are not afraid. These men must love gold above all else. They must love it so much they will die for it if need be."

With alarm, Jesus pushed his chair back and stood by the table. "But Maria, I know of no such men. I would—"

Eyes ablaze with gold fever, she cut off Jesus. "It's so obvious. This is the only way, the only chance I have to save the land. I will find the men we need, wherever they may be and then ... *then* I will find La Dura!"

CHAPTER EIGHT

NOGALES, MEXICO WAS A JUNGLE OF DECAY, A MIX OF flashing neon, tawdry hotels, crumbling arches, peeling walls, twisting alleys with large rats running over endless heaps of garbage.

A four-wheel drive slowly came up the dark street and stopped in front of a fleabag called *La Macarena.*

La Macarena was a filthy place with a lone light bulb over the fading sign. Maria got out and indicated that Jesus was to stay in the car. She entered through the broken door. Music from a cantina—the song was "La Paloma"—followed her into the dimly lit lobby. A very pregnant woman was sitting behind the dirty counter, fanning herself with a broken fan.

"*Señora,* I am looking for a man named Flynn O'Neil; is he here?"

The clerk took a long look at the beautiful woman wearing expensive designer jeans with a low-cut sport shirt that revealed the tops of creamy breasts. She parted her thick lips and her blackened teeth passed as a smile. "Flynn must have come into some pesos. The women he buys are not so expensive as you."

The comment made Maria's eyes flash. "I'm not

for sale! It's Flynn who's going to be bought. Now, where is he?"

The thick lips closed tightly over the blackened teeth. "Second room on the right at the top of the stairs."

Maria started up the worn stairs as roaches scattered before her.

The woman's fat lips were smiling again. "He's drunk, as usual, so he may not be able to service you. Tell him to pay his bill."

Maria glared at the woman over the stair railing. The hall was pitch black, but the room door was standing ajar. A single bulb hanging by a frayed cord swayed back and forth in the light breeze that blew through the open, cracked window. From the cantina, a soulful voice was singing "Reina-Reina" and it mingled with the muted sounds of the street below.

Dirty dishes filled the sink as roaches crawled over them, eating the remains. The floor was filled with a pile of empty bottles and clothes mixed together. A dresser with a cracked mirror held a half-empty fifth of cheap whiskey, and a broken chair sat by the window. In the corner stood an ancient bed with dirty sheets, half dragging on the floor. Lying on the bed was the naked body of Flynn O'Neill, an over-the-hill mercenary who had answered the ad Maria had placed in a border paper.

He was sleeping a drunken sleep, mouth open, snoring. His sandy hair was shot with grey and his still handsome face was covered by a week's growth of beard. Although he had abused it, his six-foot, two-inch body was still hard and powerful.

Maria's nose curled at the stinking smell of this place. For a long, hard moment she stared at the panorama before her, and then flung the door closed. The smash of wood brought Flynn's head up off the bed. His bleary, red eyes tried to focus on this vision of beauty that had come into his world.

"What the hell's going on? Who the hell are you?"

He stumbled from the bed, trying to orient himself. He saw the uncapped whiskey bottle on the dresser and poured the remaining liquid into a filthy glass.

With a swipe of her hand, Maria knocked the glass from his fingers and it flew across the room, shattering on the iron leg of the bed. Flynn watched in horror as the contents spilled over the floor. He recovered and advanced on Maria, his fists clenched. She never gave an inch. Flynn was having trouble focusing.

"Just a second, what do you think you're doing? Who in the hell are you anyway?"

"Just calm down, Mr. O'Neill. I'm Maria Ropero. You answered my ad and said you wanted to work for me."

Flynn was still trying to get it all together. "You mean you're the one who is looking for someone to go on a treasure hunt? Woman, this is the twenty-first century."

Maria couldn't help but smile as she watched Flynn trying to fight his way out of his booze-induced haze ... while standing in front of her with his well-endowed manhood exposed.

"Mr. O'Neill, if you have a pair of pants, I would suggest you put them on, and then maybe I can clear up a couple of things for you."

Flynn looked down and realized for the first time that he was stark naked. He stumbled, making his way to the broken chair and grabbing a dirty pair of jeans. He stuffed his legs into them and pulled the zipper shut before turning around.

"Mr. O'Neill, you must understand that there are places where the clocks of time have not moved for centuries and this is that kind of place where we must travel. By the way, this is not a treasure hunt, as you put it. I have the *only* map to what may be the greatest storehouse of riches the world has ever known. There are bars of gold and silver and sacks of gold coins."

Flynn could hold back no longer. "There is only one place like that in the entire world and it has been lost for centuries. No one knows how to find La Dura!"

Maria's eyes burned into Flynn like lasers. "Wrong, Mr. Flynn. Not only do I know how to find La Dura, I'm going to find La Dura. Tomorrow, when you feel better, we'll discuss the deal. I'll be expecting you at 7:00 p.m. at the Cattleman's Club in Tucson."

Wheeling around, she pulled the door open, then slammed it behind her. The room was silent, then from the cantina a soft guitar played "Mi Vida".

CHAPTER NINE

FLYNN HEARD THE CRY OF GULLS AND THE THUNDER of the ocean's surf. Then he saw the gray water and the puffs of low clouds brushing the white-frothed tops of the waves. A woman was walking down the beach and the mist made it appear that she was somehow suspended over the sand, but then the mist tore free and the woman was walking on the sand again.

Coming closer, she picked up a stone and threw it over the water and watched it skip. At that instance, the sun burst over the mountain and its light streamed along the beach, licking the rocks and sand. A breaking wave thundered white on the beach and foamed around the woman's ankles. As she stood still, the water rolled back to the sea.

Her blond hair took on the rays of the sun and formed a halo. She came closer. He watched her well-formed body moving in the white linen dress, water swirling over bare feet. Her perfect features were touched by the blush of the sun. Was ever a woman more beautiful? Then, she was a heartbeat away. She smiled. Perfect white teeth framed by ruby lips.

"Darling, now that you've thought it over, you're going to forget all the silliness about entering the military. My father will get you an executive job, handling government contracts."

This was the way the nightmare always started. Like trying to run under water ... like a dream where you struggled to escape, but everything you did was in slow motion while those in pursuit ran at top speed.

He took her gently in his arms and tried to make her understand that he had to make the current war *his* war. He owed his brother that much. Don was not only a brother, but his best friend. He had been captured during a firefight in the Middle East, tortured by Al Qaeda, and died in that faraway part of the world.

He also owed something to America and, the way things were shaping up, his country needed him and he had to answer the call.

Yes, he loved her more than anything else in the whole world. All he was asking was that she wait for him. Then they could marry and have a lifetime together. Their love was so complete it could easily stand the strain of a few months or a couple of years while he did what he had to do.

She disengaged herself from his arms. She told him she would not wait, that whatever they had between them was over.

"You want to be part of this senseless adventure so you can be an officer. You want prestige. All this because you're from a poor background; you feel you can attain this on your own rather than let my father place you where you will make a great deal of money. He can see to it that you are granted power, wealth, and position beyond your wildest dreams. We can own a dream house and mingle with the movers and shakers in society. You came from nothing and staying nothing is your desire."

Turning, she started back up the beach, back toward the big white house sitting at the foot of the mountain, visible now that the mist had cleared.

He watched until she faded into the distance and then there was nothing but blue sky, white sand, rolling surf, and the cry of gulls.

"Nicole! Nicole! Come back, come back," he cried, but his voice was lost in the wind.

———

Flynn sat bolt upright among the tangled sheets, sweat drenching his body. It was always the same— the nightmare, reaching for the impossible.

She had not waited. Six months later she was married in what was called by the press "the event of the season" and he was an Army Ranger First Lieutenant headed for a hell called Iraq.

When he was wounded and hovered between life and death, burning with fever, the nurses said he had called her name.

He had whispered her name and looked at her tattered picture in the blazing desert where his men died and replacements soon followed in their footsteps.

During his tour of Afghanistan, he was decorated with the nation's highest honor. He wondered if she knew. Was she proud of him? Did it make any difference? In her sheltered, moneyed world, what did the reports from the battlefront mean?

At last it was over and he came home. Home to a nation wondering what had happened. Two wars we should never have been involved in, but wars we should have won.

He walked the beach and saw, from a distance, the big white house at the bottom of the mountain. In the village, he was told that the woman and her husband were gone. They had homes in other places in the USA, as well as other countries.

Despite what he knew to be true, something made him stay. He dreamed that one morning, when the sun burst over the mountain; he would find her on the beach. They would embrace and kiss and all the time between would vanish and they would be together forever.

At last, he realized this was only a dream. One dream that could never come true. So he left and drifted to Africa and a dozen other political hot spots. No matter what the economy of the world might be, there were always well paying jobs for talented mercenaries whose existence was made up of burning villages, stinking jungles, high-risk assignments and, in time, death.

Slowly he got out of bed and walked to the broken window and pushed it up. Sitting on the windowsill, he looked out over the darkness of Nogales and thought about the beautiful woman who had been in this very room just hours ago.

Could it be possible, after all that had gone before, he could find a new love, something that would last? Or would it be like all the other dreams, tossed into the trash can of despair?

The faint light of dawn streaked along the east when Flynn at last left his window seat. There was something about him now that wasn't evident earlier: the spring in his step, the look in his eye.

Maybe this would be different. Maybe the search

for La Dura would bring the answers he had been looking for.

In the Far East, they believed that every living soul had a destiny. Maybe La Dura was his.

CHAPTER TEN

Wɪᴛʜ ᴛʜᴇ ʀᴀɢ-ʟɪᴋᴇ ᴛᴏᴘ ᴅᴏᴡɴ, Fʟʏɴɴ ᴅʀᴏᴠᴇ ᴀ convertible that had seen better days. The volume of the radio was high as he listened to Marty Robbins singing "Raindrops on My Window, Teardrops in My Heart."

What a change in Flynn. He was wearing "dress up" clothes: a blue blazer over a crisp white shirt and gray slacks. He was freshly shaved, which was a 500% improvement over the night before. It was evident he was in a happy mood.

He turned through the gates into the parking lot of the Cattlemen's Club, where an attendant wearing a white jacket with gold trim gave him a ticket, and slid behind the wheel taking his battered car away to be parked in the company of new Jaguars, Cadillacs, and several Rolls Royces.

Flynn entered through the carved doors. The dark interior enveloped him. This place spoke of old money. A small group of men in golf clothes played Liar's Poker at the bar. At the dimly lit tables, men were dressed in expensive western suits, and women were showcasing their charms in summer cocktail dresses.

"May I help you, sir?"

The deep voice of the host brought Flynn back to reality.

"Yes, my name is Flynn O'Neill. I'm looking for Ms. Maria Ropero."

"Right this way, sir. Ms. Ropero is expecting you."

The host led the way through the plush club to a table where the beautifully gowned Maria was seated with two older men. One was overweight with dark blond hair, and although he had a ready smile, something told you he could be very hard.

The second man was obviously Hispanic and reminded Flynn of the old time film star, Gilbert Roland. Maria's eyes sparkled with approval of the new Flynn. "Good to see you, Flynn. We came a little early to talk business. Flynn O'Neill, this is my attorney, Randolph Hansen."

Flynn shook hands with the man with the dark blond hair,

"My pleasure, Mr. O'Neill."

Maria introduced the Latino as "my financial advisor, Jose Alvarez".

Alvarez extended his hand. "*Señor*, it's my pleasure."

The waiter arrived with a round of drinks.

"Flynn, we ordered before you arrived. What would you like?"

"Make it a tall iced tea."

Maria had a quizzical look in her eyes as the waiter took Flynn's order.

"Mr. O'Neill? Or may I call you Flynn?"

"Please do, Mr. Hansen."

"Just call me Randolph. When Maria's father was alive, our law firm handled both his personal and business affairs. When my father died, I became head of the firm and we were retained to help guide the destiny of Maria's holdings. It is sad to say that the economy of the past few years and present world conditions have not been kind.

"I have brought Maria an offer from an eastern company to buy her land and develop a five-star resort, country club, and luxury housing on her spread. To date, Maria will have none of that. However, no matter what conditions are or will be, I have gone on record with Maria, recommending that she forget this trip to Mexico and her wild fantasy of finding treasure in this lost La Dura."

Alvarez had been listening to Hansen's speech and cut in. "I have been associated with the Ropero family even longer than Mr. Hansen. My grandfather and father were financial managers before me. Of course, I have heard all the legends, all the songs and stories, the mixing of fact and fiction that passes for the history of La Dura. I have told Maria that any trip into Mexico to search for treasure is an invitation to destruction."

Hansen was squirming in his seat, waiting to dominate the conversation. "If I would condone this, which I do not, the legal ramifications are endless. If there is such a place as La Dura, which was supposed to have been a storehouse for a series of mines controlled by Jesuit padres, a contract would have to be worked out with the Vatican, since they would have a claim to at least half of any treasure found, not to mention what would belong to the Mexican government."

"Excuse me, Mr. Hansen," interrupted Alvarez. "I want to point out to Flynn that, apart from the legal aspects, I would be terrified to think what might happen to a woman alone in an area of the world that defies the use of high-tech equipment of any kind. A four-wheel drive, helicopters, or modern mining equipment mean nothing. This area is as remote from the world as it was in the 16th century. Only horses or mules can be used, otherwise one must walk. The land is a killer. It's desolate, rugged country."

Hansen came to his feet. It was evident that, for him, the conversation was over. "Believe me, Flynn, I have done everything in my power to stop this venture before it begins. Maybe you can make Maria understand that a crazy scheme like this will only end in disaster."

Alvarez stood and kissed Maria's hand. "I am sorry we have to leave, but business never waits. I know the pain in Maria's heart, but maybe the time has come to sell the land and for Maria to start a new phase in her life. The one thing I do know is that she must forget La Dura. Otherwise ... well, enough said."

Alvarez and Hansen moved through the Club, stopping at several tables, shaking hands and greeting friends and business contacts.

"Waiter, bring us two champagne cocktails." Maria turned to Flynn. "Well, I wanted you to hear the experts, or at least those who claim to be experts. Alvarez, I understand. He has been a part of the Ropero fortune ever since he was born. Hansen, well, I remember his father and they are so dissimilar, it's hard to believe that Randolph is his son. So, the experts have given their opinion. Now, Mr. O'Neill, are you with me or do you want to forget you ever heard about La Dura?"

Flynn leaned back and looked into the sparkling eyes. He admired the smooth white shoulders, the well-formed arms and the long tapered fingers. He watched the rise and fall of her breasts smiled slowly. "I'm with you Maria, all the way."

The waiter arrived and served the champagne cocktails with a cube of brown sugar dissolving at the bottom.

Flynn raised his glass. "To the future."

Maria raised hers and looked deep into Flynn's eyes. "To La Dura."

Maria toyed with the stem of her glass. "Now that you have heard the whole story, do you think you can find men who will go to La Dura?"

"I can find them. You won't like them and, for that matter, neither will I. The kind of men we will get are hired guns. Speaking of guns, it is against the law for visitors to have guns in Mexico."

Maria's eyes flashed fire. "I don't care what the law is. We are going to have guns. You are going to get the men, and we're going to find La Dura!"

A very relaxed Flynn let a long moment go by before he spoke. "Maria, if I could have just one wish on this beautiful Arizona evening, I wish I would have met you before you ever knew about La Dura."

The band had started playing a soft rhumba version of "Maria Elena".

"Ms. Ropero, may I have the pleasure of this dance?"

They moved to the dance floor where Maria slipped into Flynn's arms. They seemed to fit together like they were made for each other.

"You know, Flynn, I would have never guessed you could be so charming or such a wonderful dancer after our introduction last night. It must be taking a great deal of effort to keep away from the hard booze."

Flynn waited a heartbeat, then looked into her

eyes. "Like Mr. Alvarez said, maybe it's time to start a new kind of life."

Slowly, they danced to the romantic music. Their bodies molded as they swayed to the sensuous tempo.

As the song was ending, Flynn's mouth was close to her ear and he whispered, "Maybe there is something in life that is more important than anything we have ever known, even more than the gold of La Dura."

When the music ended, they were pressed tight together, his lips against her hair.

CHAPTER ELEVEN

Bright morning sunlight splashed the table and bounced off the silver service where Maria was seated on the veranda of the Ropero ranch house.

Randolph Hansen was half out of his chair. His face was twisted with fury, veins bulged in his neck, and his skin had turned a mottled red. He pounded the table with his fist. "No! No! No! This is insane! This is utterly unacceptable behavior. A grown woman, a woman who should be thinking of marriage and bearing children instead is following a crazy, impossible dream. No, not even a dream, a fantasy ..."

Maria's response was straight to the point. "My father was no fantasy; he found La Dura."

"Yes, your father and his crazy schemes." Randolph sneered. "If Francisco Ropero would have paid attention to his ranch rather than running amok with gold fever, he would be alive today."

Hansen pulled a sheaf of legal papers from his overstuffed briefcase as he plunged on. "I don't want to hear any more of this nonsense. I want you to sign these papers so that the deal with the development company can move forward."

Maria pushed her chair back roughly, and stood. "I've heard quite enough. I am not signing my ranch away. It is all I have in the whole world. My father's legacy is the ranch and the maps he left me. He left them to be used in a time just such as this."

A ragged giggle escaped Hansen. Hysteria hung in the air. "Yes, he left maps with an Indio. That should tell you how competent your father was."

"Jesus is loyal and true, and his family has been a part of ours forever. He cares about me, the ranch, everything."

A tic twitched at Hansen's cheek, like a worm under the skin. A giggle rasped through his voice. "Don't insult me by telling me what he cares about. Open your eyes. I am the person who cares about what happens to you, and you're not going on this crazy adventure."

"I have Flynn to head this expedition and I'm going!"

The veins in Hansen's temples were swollen and pounding, and his face was taking on a dark red hue. The tic in his cheek became more pronounced. "Please spare me a lecture on Flynn O'Neill. I know all about his military heroics, but what about the time since the war? He's been a mercenary, a soldier of fortune, a drifter ... just a plain bum."

Maria looked hard at him. "Did you ever stop to think that maybe he hasn't found what he's looking for in life? That maybe he is seeking something ... something that he can hold onto?"

Randolph Hansen closed his briefcase with a vicious snap. "He's seeking, all right. He's seeking your money. He's as crazy as you are to even think of being part of this."

Randolph stopped short and presented a different face to Maria as he choked back the hysterical giggle in his throat. He was starting to unravel. "Maria, darling, let's not quarrel this way. Let's forget this entire conversation and talk about a future—"

The scream of tires sliding across the driveway gravel cut off Hansen. Flynn killed the engine and stepped from his ancient convertible.

"Good morning, Maria. Morning, Randolph."

Hansen stomped down the porch steps, head down. Without a word, he passed Flynn and threw himself into his Mercedes, started the engine and, in a hail of gravel, whipped down the drive.

Flynn watched the big car speed into the distance. Maria's words snapped his head around.

"Where have you been? You're an hour late and that's something I won't tolerate. After all, I'm your employer and I expect you to be on time. Do you have the men and equipment?"

A bewildered Flynn stood at the bottom of the steps, turning his hat in his hands. He was serious and more than a little hurt by Maria's anger.

"Everything is ready, but I've been thinking, maybe you should give a little more

thought to the opportunity to sell your land. They are offering an awful lot of money. Why you could afford to do anything, go anywhere."

Maria gritted her teeth. "Mr. O'Neill, let's get one thing straight. This is *my* land and La Dura is *my* treasure, and I intend to have them both."

"All right, Ms. Ropero, we'll do it your way. I'll meet you in Mexico a week from tomorrow as we planned." Flynn squared his hat on his head and turned toward his car when Maria's voice brought him up short.

"Flynn, why were you late this morning?"

He turned and slowly walked back to the foot of the stairs.

"I was at the library."

Maria was astonished.

"What were you doing there?"

"I pulled out some old newspaper files and found some interesting reading about a beautiful young lady who went east to attend Greenbrier College for Women and then on to Harvard, where she earned a degree in Business Management. At one time, she was engaged to millionaire Colt Ransom, one of the Kentucky Ransoms, famous for their race horses."

Maria had a soft, dreamy look and spoke in a quiet voice. "That was a lifetime ago."

Flynn reached up with one hand and covered Maria's hands resting on the porch railing. "I wish I could have been a part of that lifetime. I would have liked very much to have known that girl, but in this lifetime, I'm very happy to be with you."

For a heartbeat, they remained as they were, then Flynn took his hand away and slowly walked to his car. The engine kicked over and he made the turn in the circular drive. Long after the cloud of dust had vanished, Maria remained standing in the same position, her eyes on some distant horizon that only she knew.

CHAPTER TWELVE

LAS VEGAS. NEVADA

SHE THOUGHT SHE KNEW ALL THE SIGNS. THOUGHT she could read men like an open book, but she had guessed wrong this time. She knew he would be rough. She'd taken on rough men before, but this man was an animal and now she was paying the price.

She first saw him pressed up against a craps table, his wide, powerful shoulders covered by a dark linen sports jacket, his white slacks immaculate. His swarthy face was closely shaven, his jowls a heavily shadowed bluish color that came from a twice-a-day need to shave. The white slash of a scar running down one cheek only accented the darkness of his skin. He was winning and winning big. He moved his two-hundred-and-forty well-muscled pounds with ease, jostling players on each side.

One started to make a remark, then read the danger signals in the hooded dark eyes.

She made eye contact when he looked up from the red chips that were piled in front of him. A simple nod indicated that she should wait. After cashing in, he joined her at the bar, where he ordered a scotch and water, bought her another drink, and left a sizeable tip.

He let his gaze move slowly over her. She looked to be about twenty-five. Short blond hair, full breasts encased in a green halter. Tiny waist, nice flaring hips in white shorts, and good legs. Pretty face with soft full lips. He knew there were a million of these broads in Las Vegas, but this one could be interesting and he was feeling a warmth in his groin. He wanted to spread her out, mess up her cool good looks, and let her know what a bull of a man he was.

"Are you a guest here at the Mirage?" she asked.

"I always stay here when I'm in Vegas."

"Will you be here for a while?"

"No, I came in from Colorado the first of the week and I'm leaving for Mexico early in the morning."

"You want to party?"

He looked at the gold Rolex buried in the curly black hairs of his wrist, then back at the girl.

His eyes were black slits, boring into her, making her feel off the wall and a little afraid. "Three hundred for the night.

Five hundred is my fee for all night."

"Hell, it's after one already. Three hundred, take it or leave it."

She knew the chances of landing a five-hundred-dollar trick during what remained of the morning hours was slim and, what the hell, this guy might give her a good toke.

"Okay, three hundred. Your room or my place?"

"Why would I leave the comforts of home? Let's go." He took her arm and guided her through the crowd, past the big tank where a variety of fish swam in endless circles behind the registration desk, and onto an elevator that took them high up into the hotel. Getting off, they walked down the thick carpeted hallway to his suite. He inserted his card key in the lock, opened the door, and pushed her inside.

A big trunk stood open in the living room. It was packed with expensive clothes, suits, jackets, slacks, and fancy shirts.

"That trunk looks like you're going abroad."

"I told you, I'm headed for Mexico and where I'm going, I'll have no use for these. The hotel will store them until I come back." He reached in his pocket and pulled out a thick wad of cash. He peeled off three one-hundred-dollar bills and handed them to her.

She put them in the little bag she carried. He took her by the arm and led her into the bedroom where she put her purse on a dressing table that held a pair of gold cuff links, a money clip with neatly folded hundred-dollar bills and a folder containing airline tickets.

"Okay baby, get naked. You're getting paid to work."

"May I use the bathroom?"

"Yeah, just don't shut the door."

He walked to the phone, picked it up, and carried it to where he could see her while she undressed.

"Give me the Bell Captain. Hi, this is Cory. Yeah, you should know my room by now. Listen, I'm leaving at five-thirty. My trunk and bags will be packed and ready to store. I'll leave a stamped envelope on top the trunk. Just send me the claim check. I'll be back in a month or so, and I'll see you then."

The woman was naked now. She stood in front of the basin washing between her legs. He admired her lush buttocks. She took a towel and wiped herself dry, then turned and walked into the room.

Her breasts were perfect. High, with pink
nipples already erect. Her hips swayed when she
walked and at the bottom of her gently rounded
belly was a bush of blond curls.

He whistled. "Well, a natural blond. What do you
know?"

She walked away from him and sat on the edge
of the king-sized bed.

He felt fire flash in his groin and his hardness
sprang to attention. He snorted and tore the shirt
from his body, which was matted with black hair as
he flexed his muscles.

The girl felt a quiver of fear at seeing the powerful arms and shoulders. Turning away, he slid his
expensive slacks down tight buns, hairy legs, and
well-muscled thighs. He tossed the pants onto a chair
and pulled his briefs down to his ankles and kicked
them loose. When he turned, her breath caught in
her throat. She had men who were well-endowed,
but nothing like the length and thickness that was
pointed at her.

He advanced to where she was and, with a light-
ning-quick move, grabbed her by the back of her
head and forced her face into his waiting groin.
There was no time to check for spots, scabs, or
rashes, or to say anything about a condom. He was
forcing his huge member between her soft lips, gagging her and causing her to choke. Tears ran from
her eyes and she tried to push him away, but he put
more pressure on her head.

"Oh, my God! Oh, my God!"

He grabbed her hand and put it on his testicles.
She attempted to gently rub them and his hairy buttocks but she was choking and dying from lack of air,
and he was laughing. The laughter was the last thing
she heard before she fainted.

She gradually awakened and realized that she ached in every part of her body. Her hips and buttocks felt as if they were split. Her legs were raised high with her knees bent back beside her head. Her sore crotch was being ripped as the animal thrusted his huge member deep into her belly. She tried to scream, but a meaty hand rocked her head with a vicious slap that split her lip. She whimpered and tears trickled down her puffed and swollen cheeks.

With his weight forcing the backs of her thighs toward the bed, he grinned as he took inventory of her abused body. The lovely breasts had darkening bruises where his huge hands had ravaged her. Teeth prints were around her nipples and on the softness of her belly. He looked down, watching his manhood drive in and out through the tangle of blond curls now wet with sweat and semen.

"You little whore, you'll never forget the ride Cory is giving you. You won't be peddling your ass for a while after having a *real* man."

The girl groaned and silently prayed that God would release her from the pain.

His powerful thighs bunched as he felt a mighty rush and once again he drove to the hilt and released deep in her body.

He let his weight settle on her as he rested.

Looking at his watch, he grunted and slowly withdrew, then rose from the bed. Without a backward look, he went to the bathroom, closed the door, and in a few seconds the sound of the shower broke the silence.

The needle spray beat his shoulders and brought a feeling of well-being and rejuvenation. He lathered his hairy body with a thick coating of soap and felt a soft flash of fire as he washed his genitals and re-membered how surprised he was that a woman of her profession was so tight. He would have liked to have had another session with her, then taken the straight razor and long-handled pliers from his travel bag and inflicted exquisite pain, but there was no leeway in his schedule. He was booked on the only flight that could get him to Mexico on time to make the rendezvous.

He cut the shower and reached for one of the thick towels.

She was lying in the fetal position, quiet as death. The big trunk was packed, lid closed, and a self-ad-dressed envelope plus two one-hundred dollar bills lay on top. Cory dressed in a western shirt and slacks, and an expensive pair of snake-skin boots encased his feet. His face was shadowed by a black cowboy hat.

"Come on you little whore. Get up and get out of here. I have a plane to catch."

She moved slightly and rolled over on her stomach.

"I told you to get your ass up and get out of here."

There was no movement from the bed. Cory ripped his wide leather belt from his pants and with a powerful swing came down across her lush buttocks, the belt making a purple streak.

"Aghhhh." The girl twisted and turned and tried to rise. Another slash of the belt caught her across her thighs and another followed across her shoulders. She rolled off the bed onto the floor.

"Please, please don't hit me again, I'm going."

He threw her shorts, panties and halter to her. "Make it fast."

Aching from head to toe, she fought her way into

her clothes, picked up her sandals and purse, and headed for the door. Her hair was standing in spikes and her face had purple and green bruises, and a black scab was forming on her lip as the first rays of sunlight filtered through the drapes.

Cory grabbed her arm with one hand and a small travel bag with the other, then pulled her down to the elevator. He looked at her swollen face and pointed to a fire exit.

"You don't ride down on any elevator with me. You hit those stairs and get the hell out of here."

Whimpering, the girl opened the stair door and vanished.

————

"Mr. Cory, how are you this beautiful morning?"

Cory pressed a bill into the hand of the baby-faced doorman

"Just fine, Eddy. Get me a cab. I'm running late and I have to get over to McCarran to get a plane. I shouldn't have stopped for a bagel and coffee but I seem to have worked up an appetite."

The cab pulled up a few minutes later and Eddy opened the door. As Cory settled into the back seat, he gave Eddy a half salute and they sped out of the drive.

The cab moved into the early morning traffic on the Strip. Cory chuckled when he saw the girl setting on the steps at the entrance to Caesars Palace. Her sandals and purse rested between her bare feet and she was holding her head in her hands.

The cab turned left onto Flamingo and she was lost from sight. A wolfish grin lit Cory's features. He wondered how long it would be before she discovered the three-hundred dollars was missing from her purse. Then his mind cleared and he started to think of Mexico and treasure.

CHAPTER THIRTEEN

COLUMBUS, OHIO

It had rained in the afternoon; now, it seemed that the whole world had a fresh, clean glow following the setting of the sun.

They left his mother's where they had dinner consisting of all his boyhood favorites.

They were on her front porch, gently rocking in the old swing that had been a part of that porch ever since they were students at University High. He, Edwin Morse III, was twenty-five and Eileen Claire was twenty-four. They'd become engaged during their final year at Ohio State and, now, the wedding was just four months away.

"Edwin, I am not trying to be impossible, but for the life of me I can't understand why, at this stage of your life, you have to take a trip to Mexico with this man—what's his name?"

"Flynn, Flynn O'Neil."

"Yes, Mr. O'Neil. You went down to Arizona to complete your research on J. Frank Dobie for your novel and to get some background for your poems; now you're going back to spend a month in the wilds of Mexico. Edwin, our wedding is just four months away."

He gently put his arm around her and looked deep into blue eyes that sparkled in her lovely face. "Eileen, this is something I dreamed of all my life. I've read about men like Flynn and I have known men like that from afar, but just once in my life, I want to live an adventure with a real live hero."

"Aren't you getting a little old for heroes?"

He laughed, a soft silvery sound that echoed off the honeysuckle growing by the side of the porch. "Sweetheart, you're right. I have no defense except this is a boyish whim and, when I return, I promise I will forget these things and concentrate on making you happy and becoming a success as a husband and writer."

She cuddled closer into his arms. "I love you so much. You know, I had a crush on you way back in the ninth grade and nothing has changed. I just love you more now than ever."

"I love you too. You're my whole world and we're going to have a fabulous life, just wait and see."

For a long time they remained silent and close; then, the chimes from Trinity Cathedral roused them.

Edwin took a quick look at his watch. "Wow! It's past midnight and I have to catch the commuter to Chicago at 4:30. Honey, I have to go."

"Edwin, I have something for you."

She reached into the pocket of her dress and drew out a small velvet bag. "This is your good-luck piece."

Opening the bag, a single gold coin fell into his hand.

"Gosh, Eileen, I didn't expect anything."

"This coin belonged to my great-grandpa Silus. He had it when he was a boy in Europe and he brought it to the United States. He said that it was blessed with luck and I want you to have luck always."

"I've got all the luck I need because I have you, but you can be sure I'll carry it every single day until I return."

They stood and he took her in his arms and held her tight, then gently kissed her lips.

"I love you, Eileen, and I always will. I'll come back just as soon as possible."

"I love you too, Edwin. I'll be waiting."

Slowly, he released her and moved down the steps. As he started along the walk beneath the big oak trees she softly called to him and he stopped to hear her words.

"Sweetheart, did you tell Mr. Flynn that your name is Edwin Morse the Third?"

His soft laughter came out of the darkness. "No, honey. He just calls me 'Poet'."

CHAPTER FOURTEEN

MESQUITE, NEVADA

THE NEW BLACK LINCOLN TOWN CAR SCREAMED across the Utah border like a demon from hell. With the tires protesting, it made a high speed turn into off-ramp #122 and slid into the parking lot of The Virgin River Inn at beautiful Mesquite, Nevada. Well, that's what the jerk on the all night disc jockey show called it. The guy who kept talking about the hubcap-sized ham breakfast. *Well, it damn well better be good.* He was hungry and, with dawn less than an hour away, he wanted to eat and get moving.

A security guard watched him as he moved toward the coffee shop inside the casino. This guy spelled trouble. About six-foot-two, a body hard as a rock, a mean pocked-marked face, faded blue eyes, and all of it framed by long stringy blond hair. It looked like he had been in a time warp from the hippie generation in San Francisco. The guard made a mental note to keep an eye on this one.

The waitress brought his ham steak breakfast and he gulped it down like a starving man. Then he relaxed with a second cup of coffee and a cigarette while he mentally sorted out the events of the past week.

The man had told him to look for the ad in the border paper and he had answered it as instructed. Flynn was a wise-ass, do-gooder with his bullshit about the military, but he would play the game. The prize was the real bait. Once he had his share of the treasure and settled his score with the man, he would head for South America. He had a fake passport and all the papers needed to vanish forever. He would have liked to have gone back and killed that fucking warden at Walla Walla, but he had bigger fish to fry.

He had fried some pretty good fish as it was. Seven men dead and the law was only able to hang him with a single manslaughter conviction. They would have never gotten him except that son-of-a-bitch Robbie Lukes spilled his guts. He tried to kill Robbie up at the pen but it didn't work out. Seems Robbie got religion, having been turned on by some cult freak. While he, Timer, was doing time in the hole, Robbie got out and seemed to have disappeared.

That prick thought he'd fake old Timer out. Like hell. It had taken three years to track him down. Just before the man turned him on to the big treasure caper, he got a fix on where the dear boy was living.

He had a nice little place in the country northeast of St. George, Utah.

The stolen pickup had glided to a halt at the bottom of a hill and careful footsteps had taken him to the kitchen door, where the screen was unlatched. He'd slipped inside in seconds and grabbed the woman from behind. Stark terror had filled her eyes when he'd told her that it was Robbie who had cost him hard time in the pen and it was payback day.

She was plump and kind of pretty. She cried and whimpered when he forced her to strip. He threw her across the kitchen table. Normal intercourse was first.

Then he sodomized her until he was satisfied. He rolled her over onto her back, gagged her and tied her down, legs spread, so that she would be the first thing her husband saw when he came through the door.

An hour or so later, Robbie roared into the drive in his new red Corvette. He was humming a tune as he jerked open the screen door. Timer chuckled, remembering how his eyes almost bugged out of his head when he saw his wife.

He rushed to her and was trying to untie the ropes around her thighs when he grew aware of Timer standing in the shadows. His face turned purple with rage and he rushed forward, which didn't show much smarts for an ex-con.

He never saw the 9-mm in Timer's hand until a bullet tore out his right knee and left him slobbering and screaming on the kitchen floor.

The rest was anticlimactic. Their kid was away with his grandma at Zion National Park and waiting around to kill him didn't add up, so after sacking the woman's jewels and a stash of one-hundred dollar bills that Robbie had put away, Timer brought the pickup to the back door and loaded his passengers in the rear. Still naked, the woman had her hands wired behind her back and Robbie was secured in the cuffs and chains that Timer had brought for the job.

When casing the place for the hit, Timer had located an abandoned well miles from anywhere. This would be their last home. He took the woman first. He led her to the edge of the well. He forced her to sit down, then placed heavy chains and padlocks around her ankles. Lifting her legs he turned her so that she was looking down the well. Both she and Robbie begged and cried for mercy ... until a backhand shut Robbie's mouth and left him spitting out teeth through bloody lips.

Tired of the woman's whining, Timer took a pair of shears from the cab of the truck, stepped behind her and cut the wire binding her wrists, then gave her a shove. The bloodcurdling scream reverberated off the walls of the well and it seemed an eternity until her body hit the water.

He dragged Robbie, crying and slobbering, to the side of the well and forced him to look over. His wife was gasping for air, screaming, trying to stay afloat, but the chains around her ankles were dragging her down and although she fought and struggled, at last she went under and all was silent except for Robbie's pleas for mercy.

With the 9-mm pressed against the small of his back, Robbie heard the gun fire, but for an instant felt nothing; then pain tore through his belly like a pack of wild rats eating his insides. He was screaming as Timer picked him up by his ankles and launched him headfirst into space. He was still screaming when the black water closed over his head and embraced him for eternity.

Timer parked the stolen pickup behind the house. It had been a hot afternoon's work. He took a long cool shower, followed by a peaceful sleep in the guest bedroom.

When he awoke, it was dark. He looked through the fridge, but nothing appealed to him except a quart of ice cream, which he ate with gusto.

He did a complete wipe-down of the house for any prints that might have been left, although he had been very careful, wearing soft deerskin gloves for most of his work.

He turned out the lights and was ready to leave when he heard a car coming up the long drive. He pulled open a corner of the drapes and watched as a black Lincoln stopped. The door opened and the car's interior lights revealed an older woman. She stepped from behind the wheel, closed the car door, and headed for the house.

Timer's eyes took a quick inventory of the kitchen. The moonlight coming through the windows spotlighted a set of steak knives in their block on the kitchen counter. He took one, turned, and silently slipped out the back door.

The woman was breathing hard as she struggled up the path to the porch.

"Robbie, Susan, we're back. Little Danny is asleep and I need one of you to carry him up to the house—"

She was seized from behind. Her neck caught in the crook of an arm that seemed to be made of steel. Her head was jerked back, jaw raised. Then came the blinding pain as a searing line was ripped across her throat. A flood of warm wetness spilled down the front of her dress. Her hands made feeble attempts to claw at the arm of steel. She fought to breathe, choked, and as she was released, she pitched forward, landing just short of the front steps. Blood gushed from her slit throat and flooded the leaves below her body.

"Goddamned old fool. Had to come back and cause me extra work."

Timer drove the toe of his shoe into the dying woman's face. He walked down to where her car was parked and ever so gently opened a rear door.

The little boy was sound asleep under an old blanket. Slowly, Timer crawled onto the floor of the car until he was even with the little boy's face. His powerful, gloved hands slowly circled the tiny throat, then came together. It was over in seconds.

He used the porch light and a powerful Coleman lantern for the clean-up. He placed the woman and all the bloody leaves on a piece of tarp he had found in the barn. He wrapped her and placed her in the trunk of the town car. The little body was wrapped in another blanket and placed beside his grandma.

Afterwards, Timer brought leaves from different places on the property to replace the bloodstained ones. When it was finished, he took the steak knife back in and rinsed it clean, then replaced it in the rack.

He turned out all the lights, locked the front door behind him, and walked down to the car. Glancing at the bodies, he slammed the trunk shut, then walked forward and slid into the cool leather seat. His gloved hands gripped the steering wheel as he started the powerful engine and the Lincoln glided forward into the night.

He mashed out his cigarette and finished his coffee. Wandering through the casino, he stopped for a moment and watched a woman in shorts playing video poker. He allowed himself a few extra seconds to admire her full thighs, and then went out the door to the parking lot, where a steady rain was falling.

He had to get to Mexico. It was going to be like old times, he and Cory playing at being strangers—until the time came to strike.

CHAPTER FIFTEEN

RAIN AND FOG SHROUDED LAS VEGAS AS TIMER turned off I-15 at the Flamingo off-ramp. Fingers of green mist, like lights from the depths of hell, filled the sky over the MGM Grand Hotel and Casino. Through the slashing windshield wipers, he saw that a great deal of the Strip was cloaked in fog and the millions of lights were almost extinguished.

Turning right onto Paradise Road, he saw the gray and maroon building that was McCarran International Airport. With the control tower framed by the stark mountains, it looked more like a federal penitentiary than a major transportation hub.

He headed into the road that took him to long-term covered parking garage and put the car into a stall on the fourth floor. He wondered how long it would be before someone remarked about the stench, that in time would come from the trunk. This was a perfect place to leave anything you didn't want. A couple of years ago, a body with a bullet hole in the forehead had sat by a pillar in plain sight for four days before security got around to "discovering" it. Some security.

He threw the gloves into a handy trash container.

The gun, the old lady's purse, and car keys went into a plastic bag. He took the elevator down to the Baggage Claim area at Level One. Anyone could wander in and out of this area without any security bothering them.

He thought about Amir Ali, his cellmate at Walla Walla. During endless nights, Ali, who was a member of some terrorist organization, described how they are going to blow up McCarran when he was free—maybe during the rush of travelers at Christmas or when thousands were pouring in for a big convention. It would be so simple.

A confederate would drive the car and park outside the doors for Arriving Passengers. Ali would stroll into the Level One Baggage Claim area with two small "carry-on" bags. Mingling with the crowd at a baggage carousel, he would set one bag down with incoming luggage, then go across the hall to the Level Two side and repeat the act. Quickly, he'd be out to the car, drive out of the airport, press the activator button and bingo! The plastic explosives would take care of the carnage. A few thousand travelers and workers would go up in bits and pieces, and the terrorists would make a very definite statement.

Timer got in line with a group of incoming tourists who were presenting their baggage tickets that matched the tags on the luggage they had shipped through. The Baggage Claim lady asked, "Do you have baggage?"

"No, I don't even have carry-on luggage, just scraps from breakfast I had on the plane." He smiled as he dropped his sack into one of the huge cans that contained the discarded baggage stubs and he moved back into the lobby. Sometime in the next hour, the bags holding all the stubs and his sack would be removed as trash, and would be sent out to be destroyed. So much for evidence.

Having time to kill, he took the elevator back to the second floor and stopped in Alejandro's for a cup of coffee. He walked over into the NASCAR cocktail lounge and had the bartender throw a shot of brandy into the steaming brew.

He grabbed a stool and for a while watched the local *Good Morning Las Vegas* show that was on the tube. A bottle-blond bimbo with dark roots, fluttering hands, and a variety of facial twists was struggling to do the weather report. When you turned away from the picture, her nasal voice sounded like fingernails scratching on a blackboard. How the hell could Las Vegas, only forty-five minutes by air from all the great talent in Los Angeles, have such lousy "wannabes" on television?

With the instinct of a wild animal, his eyes flicked from the TV screen to the passing crowd. Almost at once he saw him. Black cowboy hat, fancy snakeskin boots and western duds, he was already in character.

With the grace of a jungle cat, Timer slipped off the bar stool. He left a bill beside the empty coffee cup and joined the crowd moving toward the gate where the aircraft waited that would take him to Mexico and untold riches.

CHAPTER SIXTEEN

MEXICO – SEPTEMBER

THE OLD STEAM ENGINE, PULLING ANCIENT CARS, made its way through the mountains of Sonora, Mexico, loaded with peons who had crates of chickens, pots, pans, and all kinds of merchandise purchased at the border. Maria and Jesus pushed their way through the crowded cars and at last shared the rear platform where Jesus spoke in a loud voice to be heard above the click-clack of the train wheels.

"What makes you think you can trust this man Flynn?"

After a thoughtful pause, Maria responded. "Inside, I have a very good feeling about him, but even if I didn't, I have no choice. He was the only one who answered my ad. It seems that if treasure can't be found by planes or trucks with a lot of high-tech equipment, nobody is interested."

Jesus gave her a piercing look. "Then you told him everything?"

"Not quite everything. He doesn't know about the Medallion. Of course, having the Medallion is the key to La Dura. He does know that I have my father's maps and that I'm paying him a handsome fee, plus a share of the treasure, to get the men we need and make this happen."

Jesus kicked at the saddle lying on the platform at his feet. Awkwardly, he asked what was most on his mind. "The guns ... what has Flynn done about the guns?"

"Flynn got a pilot who flies drug runs to take him in low, so the radar couldn't pick them up. The plane landed in a cornfield field south of Guadalupe del Nocha just as dawn was breaking. The guns were in the plane, and the men Flynn hired met him there and unloaded. The pilot flew back to Rio Rico."

A mournful whistle sounded as the train started to lose speed, then ground slowly to a halt with a steely groan of brakes and the grinding clash of couplings.

Maria and Jesus took their saddles from the platform and swung to the ground. Almost at once, the train started up again and they watched the observation car until it went around a bend and was lost from sight.

Here in the mountains it was darker as the sun was fragmented by walls of tall pines, dense foliage, and underbrush. They placed their saddles by the tracks and Jesus pulled an old pocket watch from his faded jeans. "He should be here by now."

From out of nowhere, Flynn appeared through the trees. He looked as if he were ready for combat. His sandy hair and suntanned face blended well with the green fatigues that were sealed at the ankles by black jump boots. The cartridge belt at his waist carried a .45-caliber Colt automatic. An AK-47 was slung over his right shoulder. He was all business. One could well imagine that this was the Flynn men knew in the military.

"Pick up your saddles and follow me."

They moved through the thick forest of trees and underbrush for a distance of thirty or forty yards. Stepping into a clearing they saw three men and six horses. Two of the horses were unsaddled while the saddled horses had bedrolls tied on behind; the scabbards on the right held M16 assault rifles.

The men had been told they had been hired by a woman, but they had no idea it would be someone as beautiful as the creature who stood before them. Hungry eyes caressed the full breasts rising and falling under the tight black shirt, the glamorous face framed by a flat-crowned *tejano* and black jeans that covered taut buttocks and long slender legs.

Maria was shocked. What a collection. Flynn must have found them in the bars and jails along the border.

"Ms. Roper, this is Timer."

Maria felt a cold chill in her soul as she gazed at this over-aged flower child. Dirty blond hair hung to powerful shoulders that were encased in a filthy white shirt. Faded blue eyes dominated his pock-marked face, and the cruel mouth told her that this man was a first-class psychopath.

Flynn indicated a man standing in the shadows by his horse. "This is Cory."

A vivid scar ran the length of Cory's left cheek, standing out in white contrast to the blue-black beard. He was big and powerful, and his unbuttoned checkered shirt revealed a chest matted with thick black hair that shined with sweat. Everything about this man sent off signals that he was dangerous.

Flynn nodded to a man standing slightly behind Maria and Jesus. "This is Poet. He makes up our little group."

Poet stepped forward and offered his hand.

Maria took it for a brief second.

"A pleasure to meet you Ms. Ropero."

He was freshly shaven with sandy hair, and had a warm smile and a rather handsome face; he wore clothes that were clean and ironed. He was really out of place with the others. To Maria, it did not appear that he was strong enough for such a rugged trip.

"Flynn, I'd like to have a word with you, in private."

Flynn led Maria back into the forest for ten or twelve yards, until they found a small clearing.

Maria wasted no time in stating her thoughts. "Now, I understand why you didn't want me to meet this group before we crossed the border. Just where in the hell did you find them?"

Flynn was disturbed. He spoke slowly. "Where did you think I'd find them? We're going into an almost no-win situation, so there was no way I was going to get a bunch of Boy Scouts. I found them; that's all that matters."

Maria was furious. "Oh yeah, and where did you find the one you call Poet? Was he dancing in a daisy chain?"

Flynn gave a half-hearted laugh. "Poet had heard that I was a drinking man, and I'm sure you remember when I was drinking? Poet bought several bottles of good whiskey. He did the drinking, and I listened. He convinced me that he should be with me on this job. For your information, he *is* straight."

Maria was shocked. "I don't believe you. Blessed Saints, why did I ever hire you to do anything?"

A scream came from the clearing where the men were waiting.

They stopped their conversation and Flynn took

off at a dead run with Maria close behind. As they entered where the men and horses were gathered, Jesus was on the ground, blood running from his mouth, and Cory was standing over him with his ham-like fists clenched. He snarled and aimed a kick at Jesus' head, but Flynn caught Cory with a shoulder jab and sent him staggering off balance as Maria ran to Jesus and knelt down by his side.

"Cory, what the hell is going on?"

Cory acted like a huge animal in a rage. Spittle was on his mouth and his eyes were rolling as he moved back and forth. "I don't ride with any stinking Indio. They are dirt ... worse than dirt. They are—"

Maria pushed Flynn aside and came face to face with the enraged Cory. "Let's get it straight, Mr. Cory. I'm paying your salary and I'm cutting you in on a share of the treasure. If you don't want to ride with my friend, then get out!"

The silence was deadly and time seemed endless. Cory clenched and unclenched his fists. His face worked as he tried to control himself, then he turned and walked to his horse.

Flynn pulled Jesus to his feet and addressed the group. "Let's get started. We have long days of riding ahead of us. Poet, saddle up a horse for Ms. Ropero. Come with me, Jesus. I'll help you saddle up. I want you to know that what has happened will not happen again."

Jesus wiped the blood from his mouth on his shirttail, and then tucked the shirt back into his well-worn jeans.

Gun belts with 9mm Glocks in the holsters were issued to Maria and Jesus. Cory sported a .357 Magnum, and his belt also held a strand of piano wire with wooden handles at each end. In addition to the Walther P38 at his waist and the assault rifle, Timer packed a crossbow with a supply of steel-tipped arrows.

They mounted and with Flynn leading the way, they rode out. Maria was second, followed by Cory, Jesus and Poet with Timer bringing up the rear, leading pack mules loaded with supplies.

CHAPTER SEVENTEEN

THE NEXT FIVE DAYS WERE ENOUGH TO MAKE EVEN the most professional rider saddle sore. Starting at sunrise, they rode until sunset with just a brief break for a hurried cold lunch. That meant endless hours on the back of a horse.

They had made very good time the first two days, but then the going started getting rougher. The scenery was becoming more spectacular. Towering mountain walls that contained various shades of red, copper, and beige sparkled in the sunlight while, off the narrow trails, thousand-foot drops into unchartered canyons awaited any horse and rider who made a mistake.

Evening camps were quiet with little talk. Poet and Jesus made simple meals and afterwards everyone rolled into their respective bedrolls and quickly found deep sleep.

Maria and Flynn had very little personal conversation. Both, however, were very much aware of the other.

On the sixth day of their journey, they arrived at a beautiful area where the pines grew down to a crystal blue lake nestled among rugged rocks pointing their spires skyward.

It was late afternoon when this vision of paradise was revealed. Slowly, they worked their way down toward the shore. The horses and mules were tired, to say nothing of the dusty, saddle-weary riders.

Flynn and Maria were riding side by side. Although no word had been spoken, they pulled in their reins and dismounted.

Flynn gave Maria a half smile. "I haven't heard a whimper from you, but I know I'm not as tough as I used to be. This is a good place to camp and recuperate."

Maria pushed back her hat so that it was secured by the cord around her neck. Her black hair was lifted by the breeze. "Six hard days of riding is enough. We have three or four more days in very rugged mountains before we arrive at La Dura. Let's take a day or two here and be in good shape for the big push."

"You're right. Don't forget, once we leave La Dura, we will head north through unchartered country and ride day and night to reach the border. By now, groups of outlaw bands know we are in the country, and although we have taken a roundabout way, once we head for the area where the treasure is supposed to be located, it won't take them long to figure what we are hunting for. We've only a short time to find the treasure house, load up, and make a run for it."

Flynn turned to the riders who had moved closer. "We're going to rest here for a couple of days, and then we'll head for La Dura."

Timer leaped out of the saddle. He was not a happy camper. "Hey Flynn, what the hell are we resting for? The little woman can't take it?"

Flynn's deep blue eyes turned to ice. "It's not your decision. This is Ms. Ropero's party and if she says we camp, we camp."

Timer fingered his loaded crossbow and Flynn slid over to be between him and Maria.

"I don't like orders, Flynn. That's why I wasn't with you goody-goody boys in Iraq. I have a feeling that, one of these days, you'll give one order too many."

He froze Flynn with his faded eyes, then turned on his heel and walked back to his horse.

Flynn watched him for a second before speaking to the group. "Everyone listen up. Starting this evening, we'll be posting guards. Figure out what shift you want and I'll take the one remaining."

As the riders moved toward the lake, Maria lingered behind with Flynn. There was a worried look on her beautiful face. Moving closer to him, she spoke in a low voice. "I think we have the makings of a major problem. When, and if it comes, I sincerely hope it won't touch you."

Flynn looked at Maria and there was love in his eyes.

CHAPTER EIGHTEEN

THE HORSES WERE STAKED OUT, MULES UNLOADED, and areas selected for bedrolls. Poet and Jesus started cooking dinner. Timer went swimming in the lake and Cory was high on a slab of rock, keeping watch. A soft warm breeze made the campsite a delight.

Fifteen minutes later, Jesus struck the stew pot with his iron ladle and called, "Come and get it. Chow time."

Timer came up from the lake. He was dressed, but his long hair was dripping. Everyone helped himself and Flynn hiked up the hill with a mess kit of chow and a steaming mug of coffee for Cory, who stood guard. After giving him his rations, Flynn sat down.

For a few moments, he watched Cory eating. Food ran down his chin and gravy dripped onto his hairy chest. He grunted like an animal in heat and spoke to Flynn with his mouth full. "You really think that little piece has the map to find La Dura?"

Flynn was disgusted with what he saw and heard, but remained under control. "I have no doubt about it. We'll all get what we've been promised. Afterwards, we'll make a run for the border."

Cory's food was running out one side of his mouth, but that didn't stop his attempt at conversation. "I'd like to get a piece of her. I bet she can hump like a wounded wildcat."

Flynn stood. He'd had enough of Cory for a while. "Forget it. It's going to take all of us working together to get the gold and get back across the border. You know as well as I do that eyes are watching us and, in time, someone will make a move."

Cory grinned like a rabid wolf as he patted his rifle. "When they do, I have something special for them. A little kiss from Cory."

Flynn started down the hill, calling back over his shoulder, "I'll send Poet up in an hour to take over, and then Timer will relieve him. I'll relieve Timer and Jesus will take us until morning."

"That stinking Indio couldn't guard anything."

Flynn turned back a couple of steps and said, "I don't want to hear any more of that, Cory. We're all in this together."

Down at the campfire, Maria finished her meal and gave her mess kit to Poet.

"You and Jesus can cook for me anytime. That was really good. By the way, Poet, I understand you have a guitar in your bedroll. Do you know any of the old Spanish songs?"

Poet practically blushed. "Well, I play and sing a little bit, but it's really nothing."

"Why don't you let me be the judge of that? I'll help Jesus finish washing up the kits while you get your guitar. Tonight, we'll have some music."

The full moon dominated the star-spangled heavens and a cooling breeze moved across the lake and through the pines as everyone, with the exception of Cory who was still on guard, made himself comfortable around the campfire.

Poet sang several old Spanish songs before he struck the opening chords of "La Dura", a song that had been sung around southwest campfires for hundreds of years.

Against the soft accompaniment of his guitar, his voice was rich and mellow. Everyone seemed to be wrapped in their own thoughts as they listened to the lyrics.

La Dura, come to La Dura,
the wind whispers from Sonora in
old Mexico.
A dream spun of gold,
jewels and silver,
into the trackless Sierra Madres
I go.

High in the mountains there
is a mine.
A legend that's shrouded in
mists of time.
There in the ruins and chaparral,
A voice in the wind, calls from afar,
like a mission bell.

La Dura, come to La Dura,
endlessly calls the breeze from the
mountains above.
I lost my dreams and La Dura,
But I found the greatest treasure
of all is love.

When he finished, everyone applauded.

A flush marked his cheeks as he stood. "You've heard my repertoire. Anyway, it's time for me to take over from Cory."

Everyone started to move to other areas of the camp where they had left their bedrolls. Poet gently put his guitar away, picked up his rifle, and headed for the hill.

Maria saw Flynn sitting on a rock, gazing across the now dark lake, and walked to where he was seated. "A penny for your thoughts?"

Flynn was startled. He turned toward her. "Funny you should ask. I was thinking of you and about my life."

Maria looked puzzled. "What are you talking about? Thinking of me and about your life?"

"I was thinking how I've wasted so much of my life, always chasing rainbows, one after the other, and never holding onto anything for very long." He paused as if hunting for the right words.

"If I would have met you long ago, things would have been very different. I just know they would. It's crazy. You came into my life, hired me for this search, one that none of us may survive, yet you have turned my life around and I've never been happier."

Flynn seemed almost desperate to get his point across. "Do you realize that I haven't touched a drink of hard liquor since that night in Nogales?"

Maria smiled wryly. "I don't think you would find a cantina anywhere in this part of Mexico."

Flynn slid off the rock and they were face to face. "I don't need a cantina. I could have had whiskey in my saddlebags. I don't need booze anymore. Being with you is the best thing that ever happened to me."

She turned and slowly walked along the lake with Flynn by her side. Maria spoke, almost as if she were talking to herself. "In a way, we are alike. I have gone with men, but in the end it has meant nothing. Maybe I've been looking for the kind of man I dreamed my father was, or maybe ... I just don't know."

"How about Ransom, the man you almost married?"

A smile played on Maria's lips as she recalled a happy time, long ago. "I think that Colt was the answer to almost any girl's dream, including mine. I met him when I was at Greenbrier College for Women. He was an outstanding student and graduated as Cadet Major at Greenbrier Military School. In those years, it seemed that Lewisburg, West Virginia was almost heaven. We dated, went to basketball games, dances, and all those wonderful events that were so much a part of college life.

"One Christmas, I visited his home in Kentucky, a beautiful colonial mansion that stood in the center of a hundred acres of blue grass, with fabulous race horses, white fences, and barns. His family was delighted and his two sisters and I became very close friends. Colt and I became engaged, but the war was on the horizon and he couldn't let that go by. After all, he was a military school graduate. So, he went as a young Lieutenant and came back a full Colonel.

"When he returned, at first it seemed that nothing had changed. He was the same wonderful, funny, strong, attractive man he always was, but I had changed. Something inside told me that my world and his were too different. His heritage was southern, with a warm social life and, of course, horses and more horses.

"In time, he met and married a lovely girl, and I understand they are very happy. He wanted me to give up my world and embrace his lifestyle one hundred percent, but I couldn't do it. My world is the southwest, cattle, and my ranch. After it was over, I forgot about love, and I haven't thought about it for a long, long time. Maybe it's impossible to find someone you can trust and love for always."

Reaching out, Flynn took Maria's arm. He turned her toward him and put his strong but gentle hands on her shoulders. "What we're doing is foolhardy and very dangerous. There's no guarantee you will ever see your ranch again. But I know one thing for sure. No matter what happens, my life will be different. Although it is much too early to say so, I hope someway, someday, it will be with you."

She looked toward the lake, then back at Flynn, the moonlight soft on her beautiful face. "I don't know what my heart knows. I can't really say how I feel about you."

She was aware of his rugged good looks, the strength of his hands, and the soft voice that seemed like a caress.

"I'm not asking for anything, Maria. I just want to tell you ... I love you."

For several heartbeats, they held their positions, then slowly, ever so slowly, they came together and their lips met in a soft, lingering kiss.

Then, Maria pulled away. She was breathless. "Goodnight, Flynn."

"Goodnight, Maria ... Maria, my love."

His eyes followed her as she walked back to the camp. Turning toward the lake, he picked up a rock and threw it into a pool of moonlight where the ripples widened and widened.

CHAPTER NINETEEN

IT WAS IN THE WEE HOURS OF THE MORNING WHEN Maria awakened. The camp was silent. The only sound was the wind that whispered through the pines. Putting her hands under her head she gazed into the starry sky.

What did she feel for Flynn? Was it possible to know a person for only a few weeks and fall in love? How about the memories of Colt Ransom that had been recalled from the distant past?

She closed her eyes and a montage of sights and sounds came from deep within her mind. Once again, she was back at colonial Lewisburg, deep in the hills of southern West Virginia.

Autumn came in many ways to many

places, but she must truly love this land because it was here she first touched the leaves with her brightest colors and this was the stronghold of beauty she most grudgingly surrendered to the cold breath of winter.

She remembered walking, shuffling her feet through the piles of multi-colored leaves, as she and her roommates made their way up Washington, then down Lee Street to Greenbrier Military School to watch the Saturday football games. It was here she first met Colt Ransom, the handsome quarterback who was the star of the Fighting Cadets. He had just scored the touchdown that put Greenbrier ahead of Culver and he came to the bench with his eyes aglow and a smile a yard wide. Grabbing a drink of water, he looked up and their eyes met. From that moment on, they were sweethearts.

Oh, what a wonderful time they had at the dances at both the women's college and the military school. Meeting at The Court, the student's hangout, for endless cups of coffee, French fries, and playing the jukebox that held everyone's favorite selections; it was a way of life.

Long walks down country lanes, evenings on Old Confederate Hill behind the college, picnics, and wading in the creeks. Christmas shopping while the snowflakes whirled and holiday music filled the air. Endless good times and being so much in love, they never wanted the school year to end. But it did.

That was the summer she visited his home in Kentucky. Its beautiful southern traditions and lovely surroundings were impressive. His family was so warm and caring. It was like being transported back to the age portrayed in *Gone with the Wind*. The endless parties, the races, the dances, the long drives through Bluegrass country, the kisses, the promises— they were all a special part of that time.

Their senior year was a whirlwind. Colt not only starred on the football team, but was Cadet Major. She was editor of her college paper and involved in so many things, yet they managed to spend every precious moment possible together.

In February, they became engaged. The thrills she felt as she watched the cadet corps at Sunday dress parades with Colt heading the battalion, his saber flashing in the sunlight ... the band playing and the flags flying ... all made her feel as if she would burst with pride.

Then came the night at the dance when he told her he was going into the army, to be a part of the war heating up in the Middle East. He didn't want to get married, in case he didn't come back. He thought it would be unfair to leave a beautiful young widow and maybe a child behind. She agreed to wait.

The Final Ball was a bittersweet event. The evening passed so fast, when all she wanted was to be encircled by his arms forever, and then it was over.

The next day at Ronceverte, she saw him off at the train station, never imagining it would be three long years until they would meet again.

Her time at Harvard never matched her years at GCW. Yes, she was in the top third of her class, won academic honors, and got her degree in Business Management, but the memories haunted her. Each night she prayed for Colt's safe return.

The summer and fall following her Harvard graduation were spent in New York, but she was restless. She missed Arizona, the ranch, Jesus, and the people she called her family. On the way west, she stopped in Lewisburg.

For four days, she shut out the rest of the world. She stayed at the General Lewis Inn where its broad white columns and long veranda echoed across the vastness of time to the gracious south of pre-civil war days. She visited the Old Stone Church and the adjacent churchyard where the headstones offered a silent history of the pioneers of this rugged and beautiful land. For hours, she walked the campus at Greenbrier College for Women with its rolling lawns, multi-hued trees, and white columned central building.

She attended a Sunday dress parade at Green-brier Military, but like her school, all the students were new, and although the flags whipped in the breeze and the band played, it just wasn't the same.

Down at the old Court hangout, they had changed the records in the jukebox and young, *really* young, people jammed the place. It was only at night or early in the morning that she could walk the streets and have the illusion that nothing had really changed. She could recall old faces and times and love remembered.

When Colt came home, they met in San Francisco and spent a whirlwind day seeing the town. That evening, at the Top of the Mark, overlooking the lights of the city that stretched all the way to the Golden Gate Bridge, they spoke about the future.

Over her cocktail, Maria watched Colt. Still handsome, self-assured, so positive of the years ahead but, sometime during that day, it came to her that his future was not hers.

Maybe it has been gnawing at the back of her mind for a long time, or maybe she had known when she returned to Lewisburg to try and recapture some of the magic and came up with only ashes of memories but, now, she was certain. There was a place in her heart where she would always love Colt, but marriage, a family, living a life in the whirl of a racing society was not what she wanted. That was his world and he deserved it, belonged to it, and needed it. It would not be right to become his wife and always want something else, so she told him.

They argued back and forth but later, as she looked back on it, she realized they had not argued with the passion of their convictions like they had in college. It was more like going through the motions.

It was polite to bring up various objections and ideas, but that's all it was, ending as friends.

After dinner they went down to Fisherman's Wharf and walked along the bay. It was there that Maria decided they should say goodbye. Colt wanted to take her back to the hotel, but she was firm. What had been was beyond forgetting, something to be remembered for always, but now was the time and place to say goodbye. They kissed, more gently than they had for years. Her eyes filled with tears. Then he was swinging down the pier, hailing a cab. He opened the door, stopped for a moment and waved, and then he was gone.

Maria walked away from the lights of the wharf and in a quiet place sat down and looked across at Alcatraz, Sausalito, and the dark hills of Marin County. It was over. She would never forget the happy years at Lewisburg, when life and love seemed the brightest. The years at Harvard waiting for Colt to come home and their world to begin seemed endless. Now they had parted, going separate ways to separate worlds and separate destinies.

A tear trickled down her cheek as she opened her eyes and once more looked at the star-spangled sky. Who would have guessed what the winds of fate would bring? Here she was, deep in the interior of Mexico, on a dangerous search for treasure and an even more dangerous encounter with love.

Sleep came slowly. She relaxed, closed her eyes, and let the wind sing a lullaby through the pines. It seemed like the wind was whispering over and over again "Flynn, Flynn, Flynn."

CHAPTER TWENTY

THE WATER IN THE LAKE WAS RIPPLING WITH SMALL circles that grew wider and wider. It was a lazy, sunny afternoon in this secluded lagoon, whose high canyon walls made it very private. Fifty yards away was a small beach where a mixture of rock and sand had been bleached white by the constant sun. Across the lagoon was a thick grove of trees. Within the shade of those trees, completely hidden from anyone on the other side, Timer was watching intently. As if in a trance, he peeled his shirt from his hard, lean, muscular body as desire flooded within and he burned with thick-throated hunger to have the woman who filled his view.

Standing on a ledge thirty feet above the water was Maria, poised, with silver drops of water from her previous dive on her lovely face. The moisture glistened on her breasts that were held high and proud with hard nipples. The water caught in the thick, dark mat of her pubic mound shone like jewels.

Flexing her magnificent legs, her body arched into a blur of white as she launched away from the cliff, suspended between sky and water, then entered the lagoon in a perfect dive. A whirlpool of white water surrounded her as she shot to the surface, then with long, easy strokes, headed for the beach. She swam to where the water was five-feet deep. Gaining her footing, she started to walk toward her towel, draped over a rock.

She was unaware of the naked outline, dark tan, except for white buttocks, coming like a shark underwater. A powerful hand grabbed her ankle and pulled her under. They thrashed around beneath the water, and then broke to the surface together.

Maria was choking and coughing as Timer had her by the shoulders. "I'm glad I stayed in camp. What a party you and I are going to have."

Maria struggled to keep her footing. "Timer, let me go. You don't know what you're doing."

The smirk left his pockmarked face and the faded blue eyes narrowed as spittle formed on his mouth. "Oh, I know what I'm doing." He pulled her tight so that her full breasts were crushed against his chest.

He pulled her toward him and the loose, sandy footing was gone and she was treading water.

"I'm going to fuck you. I'm going to get my fill of your body."

Timer felt no pain as Maria scratched and clawed.

With a powerful surge of energy, she drove her leg forward, but it missed his groin as he twisted to one side, taking the blow on his upper thigh. It was enough to allow her to break free. She turned and started swimming toward the shore.

Timer was out of action only for a split second, then his arms tightened around her waist, and he dragged her body under water. Her mouth opened and water rushed in.

With her lungs on fire, she continued to struggle.

Through the water, she saw his testicles in their hairy sack. With a desperate effort, she reached out and grabbed them. Sinking her fingernails as deep as possible, she twisted. She could hear him scream as he released her and she quickly burst to the surface, gasping for air.

Timer was holding his genitals, cursing. "You bitch. I'm going to kill you."

Maria swam for the shore with Timer behind her. Reaching the sand, she started to run.

Timer grabbed her long hair and wound it around his fist and jerked her head back. He scooped her up in his muscular arms and carried her kicking up the beach, where he slammed her on the sand and rolled on top of her. His mouth had gone slack and drool dripped from his lips. He was truly demented. Like steel claws, his hands worked over her large breasts.

"I saw you kissing Flynn last night. I'm gonna show you what a real man does to a woman."

Maria started to scream. Timer smashed his left forearm across her throat and forced his right leg between her full thighs. His erection was rubbing against her pubic mound.

Maria arched her back in an effort to buck him off and, for a second, the forearm was free from her throat. "Help! Help! Somebody help—"

The "me" never got out as Timer stunned her with a vicious right cross to the face and rocked her head back and forth with several right and left jabs.

Maria's tears mingled with the sand on her face. Her voice was reduced to just a whisper. "Please, Timer, don't do it. I'm begging you, please stop!"

Sweat bathed Timer's face and chest. His lips pulled over his teeth in a wolf-like snarl. "You're gonna beg, all right. I'm going to grind that plump ass of yours down into the sand. Now, open those legs wide and pull 'em up or I'll beat you to death."

Forcing both of his legs between hers, he spread her wide. Reaching under the back of her thighs, he pulled her legs up. At last he had a free hand to guide his erection.

"Stop it you son of a bitch. Leave her alone."

Timer twisted toward the far bank of the lagoon. Poet was standing on a rocky ledge. Stripped to the waist, his white slender body was a direct contrast to Timer's tanned, muscular frame.

"Stay out of this ass-eyes. She's mine and I'm going to take her."

"Damn it, Timer, let the woman go. I'm telling you let her go and let her go *now*!"

"You fucking pimp. You just stand there and watch what a real stud does to a bitch like this."

He turned back to Maria who was looking

up at him through swollen eyes. "Now, Baby, the stallion is going to ride the mare."

Taking his erection in hand, he slid it down her body and prepared to give a powerful thrust. At the last second Maria twisted, throwing him off balance. At that same instant, a loud splash sounded as Poet's body hit the water and with short, choppy strokes he headed for the beach.

He was a bad swimmer and his wet jeans were no help. When Timer looked back to see what was happening, Maria twisted in the opposite direction, dumping him over her left leg and onto his back. With more strength than she knew she possessed, she pulled herself up and made an effort to sprint away.

His erection was gone and, snarling like a rabid dog, Timer went after her. He grabbed her from behind, spun her, then shot a jolting shot to her face, sending her sprawling on the sand on her hands and knees.

Out of breath, Poet grabbed Timer's arm.

Whirling around, Timer smashed him in the mouth. Poet's lips split and teeth broke, and he went down. He tried to rise, but Timer drove a knee into his face, breaking his nose and sending him flat. A couple of well-placed kicks broke several of Poet's ribs.

Grabbing his hair, Timer, who was not even breathing hard, pulled him to his feet. It wasn't a match—it was just a brutal beating as grinning Timer's fist found his mark again and again.

Poet's face looked like a pile of raw hamburger. Timer drove him into a rock, and then kicked a leg. The crack of bone sounded like a pistol shot as Poet slid into a sitting position.

A groggy Maria had raised herself to her knees, her arms covering her breasts. She saw the bloody, half-dead Poet as blood-spattered Timer got ready for a final assault.

She screamed. "Stop it ... for God's sake, stop it!"

Timer was beyond any human voice. He looked down at the bloody mess at his feet. "You're not the first man I've beat to death, but I never enjoyed it this much."

Even with a broken leg, Poet attempted to jerk his body upright. Gasping for breath, he tried to push himself up the rock, but the broken leg would not hold him and he fell back to the ground. He looked at Timer and spoke through his mashed lips and broken teeth. "Come on Timer, finish me."

Drawing his foot back, Timer aimed for Poet's face, but Maria grabbed his foot. He kicked her away, and then charged the bloody bundle in front of him.

The snarl of a bullet tore a piece of the rock inches from Poet's head, stopping Timer in his tracks. He whirled and Poet's head went up. Maria, now on her hands and knees, lifted her eyes to the rock ledge she had used as a diving platform to see Flynn with a rifle in his hands.

"Raise your hands, Timer, before I kill you!"

Naked Timer couldn't believe the turn of events and was slow in reacting.

"I said raise your hands … and lock them behind your head or I'll kill you. Now, do it!"

Spittle flecked Timer's mouth. Hate tore at the seams of his face and he had to work at making his jaws move when he spoke. "You Irish son-of-a-bitch! You just signed your death warrant. This piece of shit is more of a man than you'll ever be, and this woman is going to be mine."

Jesus, a serape over his shoulder, joined Flynn on the ledge.

"Go down to Maria, cover her, and help her out of here. Take the trail behind the rocks back to the camp."

Losing no time, Jesus made his descent, sliding down the rocks. Reaching the beach, he went to Maria. Tenderly, he covered her with his serape and helped her stand.

She was crying, deep sobs coming from her very soul.

"Just take it easy, Maria, slow and easy. There's a little trail that will take us back to the camp."

Timer moved forward as if to intercept them. A bullet ricocheting off a rock stopped him.

"Just hold it, Timer. Jesus, tell Cory to saddle

Timer's horse and bring it over *muy pronto*. He's getting out of here."

Timer was close to losing control. "No goddamn wimp or Spic bastard is sending me away. I have a share of treasure coming, damn your soul to hell. I want *my* share of the treasure."

Very slowly, Flynn made his way down the rocks, his eyes never leaving Timer. As he got close, he spoke very softly. "I don't think you get it. You're through, Timer, but I'm giving you your life. You're going to ride out of here, but if I ever meet you on the other side of the border, you're dead."

Timer was seething, his psychopathic eyes glazed. In an icy calm voice he said, "I had your woman! She was lousy, she—"

Flynn's rifle butt smashed into Timer's jaw and he hit the sandy beach with blood running from the corner of his mouth. Flynn spun the rifle in his hands and placed the barrel inches from Timer's head, his finger tense on the trigger.

Timer stood still and then they heard the sound of horses coming through water. Cory was leading Timer's horse.

He looked first at Timer, then at Flynn and grinned. "I can see we had a little trouble here."

"No trouble. It's just that Timer is leaving. He has some things he must attend to across the border."

Flynn stepped back and Timer slowly got to his feet. "Has someone got his clothes?"

Jesus, who had just ridden up, leading Poet's horse, threw pants, a shirt, and boots to Timer.

He dressed slowly. Sitting on a rock, he pulled his boots over his bare feet. His shirt was open, hanging over his pants. Flynn watched him with narrow eyes. "Cory, go around and take the rifle out of the boot and unload that handgun hanging on the saddle horn. You can leave him the crossbow. Then, come over here and give Jesus a hand with Poet."

Timer's body language indicated he would like to move forward.

"You've cut me out of my share of the treasure, Flynn. You promised me gold and silver and I won't forget it. You've robbed me!"

Every inch of Flynn's being was stretched to the max. He wanted to kill this scum, be rid of him once and for all. "Mount up, Timer, and get the hell out of here."

Timer pulled the gun belt off the saddle horn and put it on. He jammed the unloaded Walther into the holster, and then swung into the saddle. He pulled his hat down to his eyebrows, started to go, then checked his horse, and spoke to Flynn. "I'm not the only one who wants the woman. There will be others. She will be taken and none of you will ever leave Mexico ... *none* of you."

Wheeling his horse without a backward glance, he rode up the hill and disappeared into the trees.

Flynn watched him leave, then walked to where Jesus was working on Poet. He had washed the blood from his face and a piece of tape held the broken nose in place. A saddle roll had been placed behind his head as he sat perched against a rock.

Poet looked up at Flynn and managed a weak smile. "Guess I wasn't quite what I pretended to be when I had all the booze back in Nogales. I'm sorry to be so much trouble."

Flynn squatted beside him. "Hey pal, we all have our limitations. If you hadn't had the guts of a lion, I hate to think what could have happened to Maria."

Poet was speaking through clenched and broken teeth, and he tried to move his body to ease the pain.

"Timer lied to you. He never had Ms. Maria. I stopped him before anything happened."

Jesus stood and looked down at battered Poet. "He's in pretty bad shape. Broken leg, nose, a couple of ribs, and God only knows about the internal stuff. He's through."

Cory was very impatient with all of this. "So, let him die here. Give him bread and water, and let's ride for La Dura. I sure as hell can't let some weakling like him ruin this treasure hunt."

Flynn uncoiled out of his squatting position like a striking Cobra. "Let's get this straight. We're not going to leave him to die. We're going to get him to a place where he can get medical attention. La Dura can and will wait. Jesus, do you think you can fix him up good enough so he can ride for a few days?"

"You're asking for a miracle, but I can try. I'll do my best. Poor guy. We can't leave him like this." He scanned Poet from head to foot. "First of all, I have to set that leg; it's bad."

"Put him together as best you can so that he can ride. Cory, if you go in a direct line southwest, you can reach the railroad spur in four days. They have medical help there who'll take care of Poet until the train can take him to the border."

Flynn took the reins of Jesus' horse and headed for the camp, leaving the extra horse behind. Leading his mount, Cory walked behind Flynn. He shook his fist at Poet and spit. His black eyes were deadly.

From his saddle roll Poet takes his phone and tries to dial his girlfriend. In this rough and rugged part of Mexico, with the high mountains and deep valleys, the phone does not work.

CHAPTER TWENTY-ONE

AT THE CAMP, MARIA HAD DRESSED. HER HAIR WAS combed and, considering what she'd been through, she looked pretty good, although her right cheek was turning black and blue.

Jesus came back with Poet. He was tied to his horse and, although every movement sent pain to all the nerve ends in his body, he was trying to keep a poker face as he held onto the saddle horn.

Cory mounted and took the long reins of Poet's horse to lead it. Maria, Jesus, and Flynn gathered around as the two men got ready to ride out.

Flynn looked deep into Cory's eyes. "Cory, it's in your hands now and we're counting on you. You know you can be there in four days. After you get our boy to the medical crew, come cross country and meet us at the village I told you about. We'll wait for you there. After you join us, we'll get new horses and fresh supplies before we start the last leg of our journey."

Poet was trying to find a way to sit in the saddle that was not pure punishment as Flynn and Maria walked to his horse.

"You hang in there, fella. We'll bring you back some treasure, I promise."

For a moment, it seemed that Poet might break down. Tears were starting to form. "I'm sorry, Flynn, Maria, Jesus, I'm really sorry for all the trouble I've caused you."

Maria put a soft hand on one of Poet's battered ones. "Poet, you never caused trouble. You saved my life and no doubt all of our lives by what you did. We are so grateful to you. You'll never know how much we care about you. We'll all get together when we come back and Flynn will bring you some treasure. I won't let him forget."

Jesus had to have his say. "You are *mucho macho*. I'm proud to be your friend."

Poet's eyes were welling with tears now and his voice was choked as he managed to get out, "Thanks … thanks for everything."

Flynn rubbed the horse's neck and looked at Poet. "*Adios, amigo,* until we meet again.

Maria let go of Poet's hand and backed away. "*Via con dios*, my friend. Go with God."

Cory flicked the reins, causing Poet's horse to lurch forward, sending spasms of pain through his body.

They headed into the desert and once out of earshot, Cory growled, "Come on Mama's boy, let's ride!"

Digging his spurs into the flanks of his stallion, they moved into a fast gallop. Soon, they are mere specks on the horizon, and then lost to sight.

Maria faced Flynn. "Can't you see that everything has gone wrong?"

"Don't worry, Maria. Everything will come out okay, just wait and see." His arms curled around her and he pulled her close.

CHAPTER TWENTY-TWO

THE PARCHED, CRACKED DESERT WAS SEARED BY THE blazing sun. The only shade for miles was a stand of *hecho* with arms thrust up, as if to support the sky. Cory, sweat dripping from his face, was standing in what little shade was available while watching Poet, who was swaying in the saddle. Only the ropes tied to his body kept him erect.

"Cory, could you help me down, please? We've been riding two days and two nights, and I can't stand the pain anymore. I have to lie down for a little while, then we can push on."

Hate and disgust were written all over Cory's face. "You weakling, I've ridden hard trying to get you to that railroad spur early so I can go back for the treasure. Sure I'll help you; try this."

He stepped forward, grabbed the main rope holding Poet on the horse, and gave it a jerk. The rope pulled loose, throwing Poet to the ground.

He ended up stretched at an odd angle, moaning and gasping for air. "Oh, God, help me, Cory. Help me, I'm all bent. Something has torn loose, please help me."

Cory knelt down in the sand and put his face as

close to Poet's as possible. "I'll help you, but first I want to know why Flynn brought you along. Is it true that you know where the Medallion of La Dura is hidden?"

Poet was in agony. It was all he could do to keep from screaming. "No, God, no. I got with Flynn one night and drank a lot of booze and told him what making this trip meant to me. All my life, I wanted to be a man like Flynn, do things like a real man. This … this was my chance."

Cory stood and eyed Poet as he might an ant. With a vengeance, he drove the pointed toe of his boot into Poet's body and the sound of ribs cracking filled the still, dry air.

"Aghhhh. Oh God, help me, help me." Poet tried to drag himself into the scrubby shade of the cactus.

Behind him, Cory slowly rubbed his fingers along the length of the white scar on his stubbled face, and then he took the piano wire from his belt. His smile was that of a demon incarnate. "Poet, old friend. God can't help you, but Cory can help you. I'm *really* going to help you."

With cat-like grace, Cory looped the piano wire over Poet's head and with all his strength, tightened it, using the two wooden handles for leverage.

Poet's eyes bulged as Cory bent him backwards. His tongue flopped out of his mouth. In vain, his hands tried to force his fingers under the wire cutting his throat. Slobbering, his face flushed purple.

Cory grunted as he tightened the wire that had cut deep into the flesh, leaving a ribbon of blood.

Poet tried once more to force his fingers under the wire; then, as if from a great distance, he heard his larynx crush. There was a dark, wet pool on the sand when his sphincter opened and his body waste spilled out. His eyes dimmed and death came with a rattle.

For a long sixty seconds, nothing seemed to move. Slowly, Cory unwound the wire and let Poet's body slump to the ground.

Putting the wire back on his belt, Cory knelt down and turned Poet on his back. He pulled the Smith & Wesson .38 from its holster and jammed it into his waistband. Next, he went through Poet's pockets. The only thing he found was a small velvet bag. He tipped the bag into his palm and out fell a single gold piece. He smiled as he stood, touched his fingers to his Stetson in a salute, and went to where his mount was waiting.

He placed the .38 deep in his bedroll, then took his canteen from the saddle, uncapped it, and took a long drink of water. He glanced at the mortal remains of Poet and watched as the desert creatures slowly moved in to explore this new attraction, alerted by the foul odor from the corpse. Ants quickly made their way toward the body while, in a shard of shade, a scorpion waited and watched.

Cory took another long pull from his canteen, then capped it and got into the saddle. For the first time he seemed to realize that Poet's horse was standing on the far side of the *hecho*. Drawing his rifle from the boot, he took aim and fired.

He put the rifle back in the boot, then turned his horse and raced away at a gallop. He was in high spirits, laughing and singing, "We shall gather at the river. The beautiful, the beautiful river …"

Riding at full speed toward the rendezvous with Flynn and Maria, the song and the sound of his horse's hoofs were soon lost and all that remained was the corpse in the dust of the desert as the ants moved in and the scorpion shuffled out of the shade to stake his claim.

Later, the evening breeze sent little dust

devils whirling across the desert, spinning and turning. As the clouds above the mountains turned to gold, there came the faint echo of a long-forgotten mission bell. The wind, playing through the mesquite and chaparral, seemed to whisper, "Come, come to La Dura."

CHAPTER TWENTY-THREE

With Flynn leading the pack mules, Maria and Jesus rested their horses on the bank of a roaring stream. Flynn had to yell at the top of his lungs to be heard over the crashing of the water.

"We're going to have to go for it. We have no choice. Otherwise, it might take us a day or two of hard riding upstream to find a better place."

Flynn pointed to where Maria should make her run, and then indicated to a frightened Jesus to travel on the far side of Maria; Flynn would take the mules and heads upstream, where he would enter.

Flynn and Maria hit the swirling waters. It took all of their horsemanship to stay in the saddle. With frightened eyes, Jesus watched them go, then sank his spurs into his horse's flanks and took the plunge.

He was no match for the river. Terror-stricken, he tried to stay on his mount. With a scream, he was torn from the saddle.

Flynn turned his horse into Maria, who was nearing the far bank, threw her the reins, and then dove out of the saddle into the churning waters.

It was touch and go as he was pulled under the raging water, and then he spun to the top. At last, with great effort and, despite a battering on the rocks, he reached Jesus and helped him to shore. The Mexican was half-drowned and Flynn was near exhaustion.

Maria made the bank with both her and Flynn's mounts, but Jesus' horse and the pack mules had been swept away.

Jesus struggled to get enough air in his lungs to function as Maria rode up with the horses.

"I tried to grab the rope to the mules, but I just couldn't make it. For a couple of seconds, my hands touched the ropes, and then they were gone."

Jesus looked like a drowned chicken but managed a weak smile.

Flynn mounted his horse, then held out his hand to Maria and pulled her up, to sit behind him.

"Jesus, take Maria's horse. We'll double up. If my calculations are correct, we'll be at the village by afternoon. We'll re-supply there and wait for Cory to join us."

Jesus mounted Maria's horse, wet but alive. They rode away from the banks of the roaring river, toward the village where they would re-supply.

CHAPTER TWENTY-FOUR

It was late afternoon when the weary riders came down off the mesa and saw, before them, huts and a few adobe buildings that passed for a village. To the south was a corral woven of branches that held two dozen horses and sleek cow ponies.

Mangy dogs barked and half-dressed children, dusty and dirty, shouted and pointed toward the riders. Old people, young men, and girls filtered from door-less shacks.

From a "great house", or meeting place toward the end of the trail that split the town, stepped five hard-looking Mexican men. They were armed with handguns and rifles. They watched with narrowed eyes as the riders grew more distinct.

The children shrank back as the riders turned onto the trail that served as the village street. Suddenly, an Elder stepped into their path. He might have been anywhere from eighty to one- hundred-years old. Standing ramrod straight, his face was creased by the lines of endless summers. He raised his hand as Flynn and Jesus reined in their steeds.

Flynn dismounted. *"Buenos días, Señor."*

As the Elder replied, it was evident his sun-baked face was toothless. "*Buenos dias.* Welcome to our humble village." His English was bad and he took his time to form the words.

Maria and Jesus dismounted and joined the group. "*Señor,* we need to buy horses and supplies. We have *pesos.* We would like to stay a couple of days as we are expecting a friend to join us, *comprende?*"

The Elder gave Maria a toothless grin as he

thought about the *pesos.* "*Si-si, señorita,* a thousand pardons, but would you and the *senor* stay at my *ha-cienda?* It is poor, but clean."

Still watching the hard-eyed men with a wary eye, Flynn answered with an amiable smile. "*Señorita* Ropero and I would be happy to share your *hacienda,* but our friend here, where can he stay?"

The Elder gestured down the street to a long, low building across from the corral.

"There is a room for sale in the back of the can-tina. Maybe your friend would like a young woman for pleasure?"

"That's up to him and the young woman." Flynn jerked his head toward the hard-eyed men. "Who are they?"

The Elder made a half-turn and glanced at them. When he faced Flynn, the smile was gone, his expres-sion grave. "'*Agentes de la ley*' who keep keep this vil-lage free from *banditos.* They also use our women and take our tribute."

Flynn's eyes grew hard. "Everywhere in the world, there are predators whose prey is the weak, the old, and the helpless." Hie gaze softened. "Enough of this talk. Where can we feed the horses, find some water to wash up, and then eat, *muy pronto?*"

Once he received the answers, Flynn took the horses to the corral. As he passed the hard-eyed men, they looked him over, then one by one, went back into the great house.

Jesus found a room in back of the cantina. As Maria talked to the Elder, he produced a large metal pan and an earthen jug filled with water he had filled from a fountain near the great house.

Jesus met Flynn coming back from the corral, and they walked to the Elder's humble home.

Life had resumed in the village, with the children running and playing, people going about their tasks, and young women taking curious peeks at the two strange men.

Flynn and Jesus washed up and, with Maria, entered the home of the Elder.

Supper consisted of tough beef shredded onto coarse plates of fired clay, covered with chili gravy that had been thickened with cornmeal. A big clay pot of *frijoles* was in the center of the table with platters of steaming *tortillas* alongside. Everyone used rolled *tortillas* to eat, deftly dipping and swabbing. The Elder's two oldest daughters, with apparent pride, stood next to an adobe charcoal hearth, watching to see that all the plates stayed full.

After supper, Flynn and Maria said goodnight to Jesus, then left the *hacienda*. They strolled through the village where carved lintels overhung weathered doors. They walked by flowerbeds that were littered with wind-blown sand and pieces of tumbleweed. Only the large fountain that stood in the center of the village seemed alive; the water bubbled over carved stones and spilled into a large circular pool below. Holding hands for a while, they sat on the rim of the fountain while the water made soothing music.

Later, they walked out of the village into the desert, where the cactus cast grotesque shadows in the moonlight. The cool breeze from the mountains had replaced the heat of the day. Wandering past the far end of the village, they came upon the ruins of an adobe house. Far in the background they could hear music from a guitar and, now and then, a peal of laughter or a barking dog. Flynn took Maria's hand again as they walked around the house and sat on the old wall facing the faraway mountains bathed in silvery moonlight.

"Flynn, what did you think of the talk at dinner about danger in the mountains?"

"You have to remember that you're dealing with very superstitious people. Most of the villagers live and die within fifty miles of where they are born. They believe that supernatural beings live up there and that they guard all sorts of secrets."

"Maybe it's just me, but I can't help it … ever since that business with Timer." Maria paused, trying to contain her words, but they poured forth like a flood. "I'm afraid. For the first time in my life, I *know* fear. Now, to add to everything else, I hear these stories about the mountains."

Flynn deliberated, choosing his words carefully. "There's nothing to fear from the mountains. It's people like Timer, and maybe that group of so-called 'lawkeeprs' or 'protectors' here in the village, or a man like Cory. *Those* are real things to worry about."

For a long time, nothing marred the silence of the desert night. Then Maria stood and moved in front of Flynn. "There's something I've never told you. In fact, I never intended to tell you, but now I know in my heart I can trust you."

She opened the first three buttons of her shirt and took a chain from around her neck, and held it in her hands. The chain held the Medallion of La Dura. It flashed in the moonlight. In bold relief the dove was trying to rise and the snake was striking, trying to ensnare the bird. Maria handed the Medallion to Flynn, who whistled softly as he took it.

"Of course I've heard about the legend, but I never believed."

The Medallion twisted and turned as Flynn held the chain away, fragmenting the moonlight; he couldn't help admiring this long sought-after piece of history. At a thousand campfires along the border, for at least two centuries, they had said that somewhere there was a Medallion, and that whoever had it would find La Dura, and be the richest person in the world.

Flynn returned the Medallion to Maria, who once again placed it around her neck. She laughed a low, throaty laugh. "Maybe you will be the second-richest person in the world."

Flynn was dead serious as he stood to face her. "I don't need any treasure to be the richest, or even the second-richest person in the world. Maria I need you. I love you and I want you to be mine for always.

She searched his eyes as she searched her heart, and then spoke softly. "I love you too, and I want you. I need you." She melted into Flynn's arms and they kissed. Softly at first, then more and more demanding; she stepped back and unbuttoned the remaining buttons on her shirt and cast it away. Her magnificent breasts were free and bathed with moonlight.

Flynn stripped the shirt from his body. His smooth chest, lean and hard, was suntanned. His powerful shoulders appeared even stronger in the light of the moon.

She came into his arms; they kissed and slowly

sank to the ground. The moonlight and the distant mountains were the only witnesses to their mating and the night was silent, except for the faraway sound of a guitar playing an old Spanish love song.

CHAPTER TWENTY-FIVE

Two days later, Flynn and Jesus were sitting on the hitching post of the cantina while Maria was relaxing on a bench beside the adobe wall.

A thunderous noise erupted up the village street. Cory was riding his horse hellbent for leather, nearly running down children, and cursing everyone in his way. His horse was covered with sweat and lather. He jerked back on the reins for a running stop. The horse reared on its hind legs, and then the forefeet dropped to the ground, inches in front of the hitching post.

Cory swung out of the saddle. He was covered with sweat and his hairy chest was filled with the gray powdery dust of the desert.

"This has to be the asshole of the world. Flynn—only you could dream up a hellhole like this to meet in."

Flynn stared into Cory's eyes. "You always have the choice of riding back two hundred miles to Arivechi if it would please you. How's Poet?"

Cory was wary. His answer came slow. "Uh-hh ... fine ... yeah, he's fine."

For some unknown reason, Flynn became uneasy.

"What did the medical people at the rail spur say about his injuries?"

Cory found himself unable to look Flynn in the eyes. "Well, they said he'd be okay when they got him to the hospital at the border." He met Flynn's intense gaze with a bold stare. "We're better off without him. We should have kept Timer with us. He's one hell of a gun hand."

Maria stepped from the bench to stand beside Flynn. "You've got it all wrong, Cory. Poet is a gentle man, a person with good breeding. Timer, on the other hand, is a first-class psychopath."

Cory flinched. "I wouldn't be too hard on old Timer. I can understand his attraction to you.

He just got all hot and bothered—"

"Look," Jesus cut in and pointed at the great house.

Turning around, they saw the *Agentes de la ley* mounting their horses. A command rang out and they turned their horses and slowly rode past the cantina, looking hard at the strangers. They drifted into the desert in the general direction of the railway spur. Flynn watched as they got smaller and smaller.

"They're on their way to loot and burn some village that hasn't paid them tribute. It's hard to believe that this still exists in the twenty-first century. Anyway, we'll be gone before they return. In fact, I want to be out of here early in the morning."

Carmen, the cantina's waitress, came to the door. She wore a scoop-neck dress that showed jutting breasts and a voluptuous figure to advantage. "*Señores, señorita*, would anyone care for a drink?"

Rubbing the thick scar on his left cheek, Cory moved up until he almost stood against the young woman. "To hell with a drink, I'd like to have you for a couple of hours."

Looking at him and smelling the stench of his unwashed body, Carmen moved away. "You *gringos* tease. Really, do you want a drink?"

Cory seized her arm and pulled her close. "Yeah baby, I want a bottle of tequila. You shake your pretty ass and get it out here, *comprende?*

Carmen pulled away, rubbing the arm that hurt from the pressure of his meaty fingers.

Cory laughed at her discomfort as she went back into the cantina.

Flynn was not amused. "Take it easy, Cory. I don't want problems of any kind. Her grandfather is the Elder of this village and we need his help to re-supply and move on."

"The trouble with you, Flynn, is that no one ever told you that women were made to pleasure men, and that one in particular could give me a lot of pleasure. Yes sir, she could give me *lots* of pleasure."

Flynn's eyes grew hard. He struggled to keep his voice low. "Pay for your bottle and let's eat supper. I want to get an early start."

CHAPTER TWENTY-SIX

THE SOFT GLOW OF DAWN FILLED THE EAST AS FLYNN and Maria mounted their new horses and rode out of the corral, followed by Jesus on a spotted pony. Cory, was riding his coal-black mount and leading three mules loaded with a variety of supplies.

The Elder had tried to persuade them to turn back. He walked beside Flynn, speaking softly. "My friend, I would not advise you to go to the mountains. Not even the *Agentes de la ley* will dare to go there. *Jornado del muerto.*"

Flynn answered with sadness in his voice. "You may be right. It could well be the journey of death, but I have no choice. It is something I have to do, a destiny I must meet." He pricked his horse with his spurs and started to move out making a salute of farewell. "*Adiós,* old one, *adiós,* my friend."

The Elder waved as the horses and riders moved away. A tear slid down his ancient, weathered face. "*Vaya con dios, vaya con dios.*" From somewhere, a guitar played the haunting strains of "Andalucia" as they faded into the distance.

CHAPTER TWENTY-SEVEN

The sun overhead was as bright as ever, but its rays were fragmented by the trees in the foothills. Cory was riding ahead, Jesus behind, leading the pack mules.

Cory reined in his horse, forcing Jesus to stop. "Jesus, what do you think? I figure we're about an hour from the village. Flynn and the woman are about fifteen minutes ahead of us."

"So, what? We better be moving on or Flynn will have our hides for holding him up."

"To hell with Flynn. Who gives a shit what he wants? It's what I want that counts and I want a piece of that little Mexican bitch back at the cantina."

Jesus attempted to push his horse forward, but Cory had his mount crosswise on the trail. "Are you crazy? Let me by. I'm riding up the trail."

Cory pulled the Magnum from his holster and leveled it at Jesus.

"Look, Beaner, I don't like you much anyhow. If you'd like to try using that piece of iron on your hip, be my guest. Otherwise, get the hell off that horse, tie the mules to those trees, and then you and me are going back for a little *puta*."

"You've got to be insane. The Elder and everyone will know the minute you ride into town."

"Ah, Beaner, you really are stupid. We'll circle the village and come up from the south. No one will see us because the cantina will hide us. We'll just slip inside and no one will be the wiser. Now, get those mules tied before I have to blow what little brains you've got out of that head of yours."

The sun was a ball of orange fire at high noon, but it was cool inside the cantina where Carmen was scrubbing the tile floor, using a hand brush and an old bucket.

Slowly, the back door opened. Cory and Jesus slipped through. Without a sound, Cory moved until he was right behind the young woman. His hot eyes traveled from the flare of her lush hips to the top of the mounds that rose above the bosom of her dress.

"Buenos dias."

Carmen's eyes were wide with fear as she scrambled to her feet.

"Well, my little flower of Mexico, have you been awaiting my return?"

Although terrified, Carmen was convinced she could get the upper hand with this foul-smelling bear of a man. "You stupid *gringo*. My grandfather will be here any minute."

Cory's massive hand locked her arm with a grip of steel.

"Let me go! I said let me go!"

Cory wrapped Carmen in his huge arms and pulled her to him. "Let the son-of-a-bitch come. Maybe he'd like to see how I can please a woman. Jesus, get behind the bar and pour me a double whiskey."

Cory pressed his lips to Carmen, thrusting his sour tongue into her mouth.

She struggled to pull away, but she was no match for his brute strength.

Jesus slid the whiskey down the bar. Cory picked up the glass and threw the contents down his throat. Some of the whiskey dribbled down his chin. He wiped his unshaven face with the back of his sleeve, but held Carmen firm with the other hand.

"Okay, Cory, you've had your fun; you've scared her half to death. Come on, she's just a girl. For Christ's sake, let her go and let's get out of here."

Cory was crushing the struggling girl in his arms, running his tongue over her shoulders, biting her neck and saying, "One more word from you, you Spic bastard, and I'll kill you. Get over by the entrance in case anyone comes in."

Jesus moved to the entrance. He wanted to go for his gun, but he was afraid Cory would beat him to the draw. He also knew that if he got to his gun first, he'd have to kill Cory. There would be no other way, but Jesus was not a killer.

Carmen tried to stay on her feet, but Cory kicked them out from under her and hurled her hard to the floor. He fell on top of her and pinned her to the tile. He tore off his shirt; his body was covered with sweat.

He pulled his lips back like a wild animal. "Quit fighting, you little bitch. I'm going to fuck you and I'm going to fuck you *now*."

Carmen was panting with exertion, her breasts rising and falling. Her eyes were rolling wildly and fear filled every inch of her being.

Cory's huge hands grabbed the front of her dress and, with one jerk, he ripped her gown to the waist. Her unencumbered breasts sprung free. Carmen screamed and at that instant the swinging door to the cantina opened to reveal the Elder.

He could not believe his eyes. "*Por dios,* what is going on?"

Carmen was on the floor, bare-breasted, with Cory on top of her, ripping her skirt. The Elder failed to see Jesus just inside the door. He rushed forward and beat Cory with his withered fists. "*Gringo bastardo! Gringo* pig! Let her go!"

Jesus leaped on the old man and pulled him away from Cory, who now had Carmen almost naked.

The Elder looked over his shoulder and, seeing it was Jesus, cried with rage and frustration.

"You! You're one of us. How *could* you?"

Jesus wavered and released his hold on the old man. The Elder grabbed a whiskey bottle off the table, raised it, and rushed toward Cory.

The man who had lived through hundreds of life and death fights was not caught unaware. Giving Carmen a shove, Cory came to his feet and smashed the old man in the face, then kicked him in the groin as he went down.

Carmen screamed again and again, alerting the villagers. Running feet hit the porch. The door swung open and two peons entered, both unarmed.

Like a bolt of lightning, Cory reached for his gun and fired twice, killing them both.

Jesus stood as if he had been struck dumb, but then he came alive. "My God, Cory, what have you done ?"

"Fuck you, Beaner. Pull that gun of yours and get ready to shoot your way out of here, otherwise you're gonna be hanging from one of the cottonwood trees."

Carmen staggered to her feet. She tried to gather bits of cloth to cover her nakedness. She rushed to her grandfather and cradled his head in her arms. His eyelids fluttered. "Oh, Grandfather, what has this dog done to you? I love you, I love you."

Bending, Cory seized Carmen by the hair and pulled her away from the old man, who tried to hold onto her. Her firm breasts jiggled as Cory dragged her along, ripping the bits of clothing from her grasp until she was completely nude. "I'm still going to have your tamale pie, sweetheart. You just come along with old Cory."

The back door slammed open and a peon with a pitchfork raced into the room. Cory fired and the peon dropped to the floor, a bloody mess of pulp where his face used to be. Two more peons crashed through the swinging doors and took their stout sticks to Jesus.

He drew his gun and fired. One recoiled back through the doors, his right eye a bloody pool, the other with a gurgling, gaping hole in his chest, slid down the cantina wall.

"Good boy, Beaner. Let's kill lots of 'em."

Jesus looked down at the pistol in his hand. He was unable to come to grips with the fact that he had just committed murder.

A peon crashed through the swinging doors and came at Jesus with a raised club. He smashed it into his gun hand. As Jesus started to fall backwards, his finger pulled the trigger. At the same instant, with the grace of a mad dog, Cory swung Carmen by her hair out and away from him, and fired. The Magnum blew away a hunk of the peon's head.

In throwing Carmen, Cory put her directly into the line of fire with Jesus' bullet. She looked with disbelief at the blood welling just above the nipple of her left breast.

Her grandfather tried to climb to his feet, but

Cory kicked him to the floor and turned his attention to Carmen, who was sinking in his grasp.

Her eyes were clouding as her lips moved in prayer. "Hail Mary, full of Grace ..."

She coughed and blood flowed from her soft lips and made a thin red stream down her belly, into her pubic hair. "The Lord is with ..."

Cory was unable to believe what he saw and he came unglued. "You crazy Mexican son-of-a-bitch, look what you've done!"

Still holding Carmen by the hair, he pushed her forward.

Pure horror masked Jesus' features. His gun dropped from his nerveless fingers as he sunk to the floor. Rocking back and forth, he made the sign of the cross. "God forgive me. What have I become?"

Cory glanced once more at Carmen and flung her dead body to the floor. Outside, voices were raised to a fever pitch. Cory sprang into action. With a smooth motion born of endless practice, he re-loaded his Magnum. He forced Jesus' gun back into his hand, then grabbed a kerosene lamp that was burning behind the bar and smashed it into the wall by the swinging doors. In a blink, flames licked the dry interior.

Jesus had not moved. He was still standing in a daze. Cory slapped his face and brought him

back to reality. "Wake up, asshole, if you want to get out of here alive. Let's make a break for the horses."

They raced for the back of the cantina. Pulling open the door, they saw the *agentes de la ley* less than a hundred yards away, riding at full speed. A hail of rifle bullets hit the building as Cory slammed shut the door and dove for the floor.

Smoke and flames raced around the interior of

the cantina. The long-dried wood cracked and snapped as it burned, making the place a small version of Hell.

Dragging Jesus with him, Cory was not about to give up. "We're trapped, Beaner, but we're going to make them pay."

———

Through binoculars, Maria studied the swirling column of black smoke in the distance. "It looks like the smoke is coming from the village."

"Something bad is going down. I know it.

Cory and Jesus should have caught up with us long ago.

Maria, I have to go back."

She lowered the binoculars. "I'll go with you. We're in this together and—"

"No," Flynn interrupted with a voice laced with steel. "I have to do this alone. Just trust me. Unsaddle your horse, fix something to eat, and then get some rest. I'll be back soon—and, remember, I love you."

He spurred his horse and headed at a gallop down the trail.

CHAPTER TWENTY-EIGHT

THE SUN HAD BEGUN ITS SLOW DESCENT IN THE WEST when the rope was thrown over a large branch of the cottonwood. Everyone in the village had gathered around the tree as an *agente de la ley* walked in, leading a horse. He halted under the sturdy branch where a hangman's noose waited.

The crowd murmured angrily as three *agentes de la ley* were seen dragging a wild-eyed Jesus from the great house; his hands were tied behind his back. He screamed when he saw the rope and fell to his knees. The crowd moved forward as he was half-carried to the side of the waiting horse.

"Holy Mary, Mother of God, don't let this happen. Save me. It was an accident, *please*."

An *agente de la ley* silenced him with a jolting slap to the face.

A small boy perched on a tree limb above the one where the hangman's noose rested began pointing wildly. "*Hijo, compañeros*, look, look!"

Down the village street rode Flynn. He was the picture of a man oa mission. His Stetson was pulled low, hiding his face; his rifle rested across the saddle.

From a distance, he could tell this was a hanging

party and not one he was going to like. When he was within ten feet of the fringe of the crowd, he reined in his horse and slid from the saddle. Looping the reins over the branch of a small cottonwood, he walked toward the crowd with the rifle in his right hand, finger on the trigger.

The crowd blocked his way.

"Where is the Elder? I wish to speak to the Elder."

An angry buzz flowed through the crowd; then, from the doorway of the great house, the Elder appeared. He required the assistance of two peons to walk. His face was badly cut and bruised. Slowly, he made his way to where Flynn stood.

"*Buenos dias*, my friend. What has happened here? What trouble has come to my friend?"

The Elder rolled salvia around his toothless mouth, then spit a gob at Flynn's feet. His face was lined with pain as he spoke. "We are friends no longer. *Terminárselo!* It is finished. Your men have done murder. Your man killed my granddaughter and the two of them killed many of my people."

"I know nothing of this. I saw smoke from the mountain and came back to help, my friend."

"No one knows how, but one man made his way through the smoke and fire, stole a horse, and escaped. If he is still on the *mesa*, we will hunt him down and kill him like the dog he is. The other one dies now!"

Flynn's face turned to stone. He indicated the branch where the rope was tied as he addressed the Elder. "How do you know that this man killed anyone?"

The Elder was very emotional. "The other one beat me to the floor and this one, I saw him kill my beautiful granddaughter right in front of my eyes."

Flynn knew he had reached the point of no return. "May I have a word with this man before justice is done?"

Turning to the villagers, the Elder gave orders to let Flynn pass through. The crowd slowly opened and Flynn saw Jesus in the grip of two *agentes de la ley*. He signaled to them to unhand Jesus so they could speak as privately as possible.

Jesus was out of control. He talked so fast that Flynn had trouble understanding what he was saying. "Flynn, thank God! I knew you'd come back for me. I knew that I would be saved. Untie me and let's leave this place!"

Flynn's eyes were flat and dead. "What happened?"

"It was Cory. He forced me to come with him. He wanted the girl and he would have had her, but she screamed. Her grandfather came into the cantina and ..."

Flynn's eyes were mere slits. "They say you killed the girl. Is that true?"

Hysterical, sweating, not knowing why Flynn was delaying taking him from this place, Jesus unraveled. "Yes, I killed her! But it was an accident, I swear!"

All emotion died in Flynn's face. "May God have mercy on your soul."

Jesus let out a bloodcurdling scream as Flynn turned on his heels and started to walk away. The crowd slowly parted to let the man with the face of steel pass.

The *agentes de la ley* grabbed Jesus and lifted him up on the horse. He screamed and twisted in an effort to escape, but they grabbed his kicking legs and pulled him so that he was erect in the saddle. His eyes bulged with fear.

The children were laughing and pointing to where he had wet his pants.

"Flynn, come back. I don't want to die! Give me a *padre*, I want a *padre*," he screamed as though he would tear the lining from his throat. "Come back, Flynn, I don't want to die!"

Flynn kept walking to the place where his horse was tied.

An *agente de la ley* put the rope around screaming Jesus' neck, whose voice box had now turned raspy. They ordered the crowd back from the front of the horse and made a sign for the Elder to come forward.

Without looking back, Flynn took the reins from the tree and mounted his horse, and slowly rode away.

"Flynn, come back. Oh Holy Mary, Mother of God, please make him come back!" He peered down as an *agente de la ley* handed a switch to the Elder, who looked at Jesus with eyes like burning coals.

The switch was raised high.

Jesus croaked and screamed, and tears started streaming down his cheeks.

"Damn you, Flynn! Curse you and curse La Dura. Goddamn you Fl—"

The switch hit the horse. It lurched forward and Jesus dropped from the end of the rope. His eyes seemed enormous and his mouth gasped for air. Twice, he pulled his legs up toward his waist, as if doing some dance of death that only he knew.

A gurgling sound came from his constricted throat and his legs kicked wildly. His face turned purple and drool ran from his mouth as he struggled to breathe. His body jerked and twitched and his bowels opened and the seat of his white pants were covered with stains as foul waste ran down his legs and dripped onto the hard earth. Finally, the body stopped jerking.

In the soft breeze of the evening, the remains twirling at the end of the rope resembled a child's battered doll. Eventually, the adults drifted away. Later, the children departed, after they grew tired of throwing rocks and listening to them thump against dead flesh.

The *gringo* rider had long ago vanished into the defused sunset.

Night came and the black sky formed the backdrop for a million twinkling stars. All was still except for the creaking of the branch as the body gently swung in the moonlight and echoes in the wind seemed to faintly call, "La Dura".

CHAPTER TWENTY-NINE

"THE MAPS, MY FATHER'S MAPS THAT WERE IN MY saddle bag are gone!"

Maria stood by her black mare, showing Flynn where a very sharp knife had cut out the bottom of her saddlebag. The top was still buckled.

Flynn leaned against his horse. It was hard to disguise the pleasure he felt knowing this deadly search for treasure was at last over. Keeping his emotions in check, he spoke softly. "That's it then. Let's turn north toward the border and head for home."

Fire flashed in Maria's eyes. "No way I'm going home, not after being this close, after all that's happened. This whole thing has to mean something; it has to be completed. I'm sure my father would have wanted it finished."

Flynn shook his head. "Look Maria, without a map, wandering aimlessly in Mexico after what's happened—and what *could* happen—just doesn't make sense."

Maria's jaw was set like stone as she threw the ruined saddlebags to the ground. "The answer is no! We're going on. I'm certain that I have memorized the map well enough to get us there." Her dark eyes blazed and she declared that they were going to La Dura. "That's *my* decision."

Flynn waited a heartbeat, and then answered with regret and sadness in his voice, as if he could see into the future. "It's a bad decision." He stepped up and into his saddle. "Come on, let's ride to La Dura."

With Flynn leading the mules, they rode through the long day, stopping only to rest and eat a few biscuits and jerky, washed down with crystal clear water from a mountain stream.

The days that follow were copies of what had gone before. Up before dawn and still riding when the sun dropped. At night, after the embers of the campfire were extinguished, they clung to each other in their warm sleeping bag, surrounded by the smell of the pines and covered by the bright cold stars in a black velvet sky.

The lovemaking was tender and long, despite the fatigue of body and soul. The flame of love burned strong. After mating, both fell into deep, troubled sleep.

It was mid-morning of the fourth day after the hanging in the village when Maria, who was riding ten yards in front, called back over her shoulder, "It has to be close. We should reach the site any second now."

She put spurs to her horse, sending up a silver spray of water as she rode through a stream and disappeared around a bend. Flynn followed. Rounding the bend, sitting among the pines, he saw what was left of an old line cabin, slowly rotting in the warm Mexican sun.

Maria had dismounted and fastened her horse to a tree. Flynn tied his horse and the mules, and started to unload.

Maria, who had been exploring the interior of

the cabin, ran to him excitedly. "I told you I had the map memorized. We're here! We're at La Dura! There's millions of dollars of Jesuit gold waiting for us, just for you and me."

Flynn held her at arm's length. "Hey, I'm the last person in the world to rain on your parade, but, Maria, to date a lot of people have suffered because of this search. God only knows who has your map, and whoever it is could be just days or hours behind us and that—"

Maria jerked free from his grasp. She was ice cold and her words came out like steel-jacket bullets. "You seem to forget my father died getting the map and the Medallion ... and how about Jesus? I grew up with him and loved him like a brother. If you want to leave, take a full share of rations and ride to the border. If need be, I'll stay here forever or however long it takes to find the treasure."

"I'm not going to leave you, you know that. The only way we'll stay here forever is to be dead. Cutting everything to the bone, we have enough supplies for one week. At that time, La Dura or no La Dura, we have to ride for the border. Let's quit wasting time. Tell me what you know about finding the treasure."

Maria instantly became a dynamo in words and gestures. "Don't bother taking stuff up to the cabin. The roof has caved in and only a small portion near the front door is livable. It's best that we select an area for our fire and, come nightfall, we can sleep there or under the ramada. Come on up to the *mesa*."

They found footholds and climbed to the long, level plateau.

Maria took Flynn's arm. "As you can see, we have two *mesas* divided by the stream in front of us. The information on the map was correct. On both sides, the walls of the canyon are crisscrossed with fake mineshafts. However, one of the shafts is real.

"Across the creek and over on the mesa to the south you see the same thing. To make finding La Dura impossible, the Jesuits had the Indians, who were their slaves, dig more than fifty fake mineshafts in the area. We have to try every last one to find the stone steps that lead to the treasure house. It could well be a shaft that starts in a canyon wall or something at ground level."

She walked him over to the canyon closest to the old line cabin. "Look at this wall of the canyon. Notice how all the vegetation grows upward? Now, study it closely and tell me what you see."

Flynn followed the rows of vegetation up and down. "There's one section, from the ground up, to about eight feet, where the vegetation grows down."

Maria was pleased with his observation. "You're right, and you'll notice this same pattern in a variety of places as you go along the walls of the *mesa*. Where you see the vegetation growing down, you can be certain that if you were to take a pick and dig in just a few feet, you would find a cave filled with skeletons of the Indians who carried the gold to the treasure house.

"You see, the *padres* had to bury them alive, in the name of God of course, because if they were ever captured and tortured, they might tell the *padres'* secret ... the good *padres* were stealing from the King of Spain."

Flynn shook his head in disbelief. "What a bloody history this place has."

Maria kept talking, never catching the depth of his remark. "If you were to open these caves, you would find pieces of the leather harness the Indians wore to carry the gold on their backs. La Dura was the center for gold brought from many places in the Sierra Madre. At various locations, the gold and silver was melted into nine-pound bars and marked with the Jesuit seal, then loaded on the backs of the Indians who brought it here. They also drove mules that carried the sacks of coins that had been minted for the religious order.

"The mines here were not as productive as some others, scattered at various places in the Sierras, but for whatever reason, this was the place the *padres* chose to hide their treasure."

She turned Flynn around and indicated the *mesa* and towering cliff walls on the far side of the stream. "Somewhere on one of these *mesas* we will find, hidden in a mineshaft, the stone steps that lead to an iron door. Behind that door is the greatest collection of gold in all the world."

Flynn was anxious to get moving and get it over with.

"As soon as I've unsaddled the horses and got the mules unpacked, I'll take the far side of the stream. You take this side and let's see what happens."

Flynn got the horses unsaddled, unpacked the mules, and stored the dwindling supplies under the ramada where they would be safe from the elements.

CHAPTER THIRTY

ONE DAY RAN INTO ANOTHER. MARIA SEARCHED NEW areas and then came back to old ones, but nothing indicated that a treasure of untold wealth was near.

Stripped to the waist, using a torch made of wood and burlap for a beacon, Flynn went deep into the earth, ever watchful of the rotten timbers that held tons of earth that could come crumbling down at any time. He climbed up the face of the cliffs to test various shafts. At times, when it seemed that something of importance might be a few feet beneath the surface, he swung the pick, swelling the muscles in his arms and shoulders, but the holes were empty. At the end of each long, weary day, there was nothing to show for their efforts.

The lovemaking, once so much a part of every evening, had stopped. The past three nights, Maria had turned in early and Flynn had taken his own sleeping bag to the far side of the smoldering coals.

The evening of the sixth day, they sat, lost in thought, as flickering light from the campfire painted their faces with dancing shadows. Flynn was sipping coffee out of a battered blue cup. Maria was sitting with her back against the cabin. Relations were very strained.

"Maria, we gave it our best shot. I'm not sure anyone can find the treasure, or if there even is a treasure." Flynn turned away from the fire to face her. "Two more days, that's it. Even if everything goes well, we're going to be mighty hungry by the time we reach the border."

Maria stood, picked up the blanket that was lying beside her, and looked down at Flynn before strolling to the doorway of the cabin. "I put my bedroll inside; I'm going to sleep in there tonight."

She started to enter, stopped, and then turned back to Flynn, who was still squatting by the campfire, the old blue cup in his hands.

"How could I have been so stupid to think I was in love with you? I wanted a man, a man like my father. He would have never thought of leaving without the treasure. You don't compare with him in any way, not in any way." She whirled and entered the cabin.

For a while, Flynn didn't move. Finally, he threw what was left of his coffee into the campfire, then slowly walked down to the stream, listening to the music it made as it rippled over smooth stones.

Raising his eyes, he looked at the dark crest of the Sierra Madres. After a while, he walked back, picked up his bedroll, and spread it out under the ramada of the old cabin.

Sleep was hard to come by. He put his hands behind his head and, for a long time, gazed at the black thunderheads skittering over the peaks above. It was hours before he fell into a restless slumber that passed for sleep.

CHAPTER THIRTY-ONE

THE CLAP OF THUNDER REVERBERATED OFF THE towering walls of the canyon. Flynn, who had been inspecting a fake mineshaft on the south *mesa*, turned away in disgust. His clothes were soaked by the sheets of cold rain, and water ran like a small river from the brim of his Stetson.

He took a few steps, then slipped in the high grass and fell into a small arroyo. Cursing, he started to rise and then realized that something felt different under his hands. Pushing away the wet grass, he squinted through the curtain of rain to see an ancient crude stone, cut in the form of a step. Behind this stone, he saw another step that lead down, then another and another.

Pulling the machete from his belt, he hacked away at the wet clinging grass and moved down six more identical steps. Everything leveled out and he was in a forest of tall grass, dripping with rain.

He pushed forward, hacking his way through the tangled web; then he saw a massive, rusted iron door covering a shaft dug into the wall of the canyon.

Emblazoned in the iron was the same artwork

that was on Maria's medallion: the dove rising, trying to elude the striking rattlesnake.

The raindrops that slid down the door looked like a million tears. Flynn tried to force the door, but to no avail. Then, near the bottom, almost concealed by thick grass, he saw a massive rusted lock, wrapped around a huge iron bolt. He trimmed the grass until he had a clean shot. He drew his Colt and fired. The lock was damaged, but still held. He fired again and the lock shattered.

From afar he could hear Maria's voice. "Flynn, Flynn, where are you? What's wrong? Flynn, answer me! Where are you?"

He carefully came up the stone steps and regained his footing in the slippery grass. He walked to the edge of the *mesa* where he could see

Maria. Her rifle was in her hands and her eyes were searching up and down the rain-swollen stream for sight of him.

She spotted him and yelled to be heard above the elements. "What's the gunfire all about? What's going on?"

Flynn cupped his hands and called into the wind. "I think you had better come over here."

"Why, what's over there?"

There was a long pause, and then with great reluctance he called out the message, knowing his world would never be the same again.

"I've found La Dura."

CHAPTER THIRTY-TWO

With a scream of wild delight, Maria dashed into the swiftly moving stream. She was almost swept off her feet but made it to the far bank. Slipping and sliding, she fought her way up the *mesa* until she stood beside Flynn at the top of the steps leading down to the treasure house. With no regard for the slippery stone steps, she ran down and hurled herself against the iron door.

Flynn, standing at the top of the steps, watched her struggle. He told her that they would have to find a stout tree limb to force open the door and that, once inside, they would have to use torches made from dry wood and the burlap sacks that had held their supplies to see where they were going.

Still gasping for breath, Maria ran up the steps, and then proceeded to slip and fall several times in the wet grass and mud as she made her way off the mound, through the torrent that was once a creek, and down to their supply deposit in the non-ruined portion of the old line cabin.

By the time she arrived back at the treasure house door with the torches, Flynn had found a tree branch to use as a lever. Both of them were soaked to the skin as the fury of the storm increased. Slashes of lightning pierced the darkened sky, and the sound of thunder threatened to tear the canyon apart.

They placed their combined power against the tree branch, trying to force open the iron door. At first it would not budge, then little by little, it moved. With a sudden scream of metal against stone, it released and for the first time in centuries, opened wide.

They moved out of the downpour into the opening of the treasure house. Their torches cut the blackness. They entered with reverence and slowly made their way down a tunnel. The ceiling was supported by massive timbers. A thin veil of dirt fell from the timbers onto the hard-packed dirt floor.

Crude stone steps took them down to another level. A short passageway followed, then more steps took them even deeper into the earth. For the first time, they noticed that moisture clung to the tunnel walls. Could it be that, somewhere deep in the earth, there was an underground river?

A crooked path took them around a sharp bend, where they were brought up short by a huge wooden door secured by an old Spanish lock. Holding up their torches, they saw ancient drawings done by the *padres* who kept the secrets of the treasure. The old lock was discolored by the dripping water of centuries and was crusted with lime deposits; however, it was no match for the Colt. The loud roar of the gunshot sounded through the passageway, causing massive clumps of dirt to fall and the timbers to creak.

Using their combined weight, they managed to move the old door a few inches. After a brief rest, they tried again. For a moment, there was no movement; then, as if released by a magic spring, it swung open wide ... into the legend of La Dura.

The light from their torches played upon a huge room. Wall mountings held four ancient tapers at measured intervals around the treasure house. Along three of the walls were leather sacks, some of which had split open and poured their contents of gold coins onto the floor. Along one wall, from floor to ceiling, were stacked nine-pound bars of silver that glinted through the musty, dust-filled air.

The entire center of this huge cavern was stacked from floor to ceiling with nine-pound bars of solid gold, their brilliance reflected in the torchlight. This horde of treasure could not be measured in ounces or pounds, only in tons. At the far end of the room was a marble altar. Over the altar hung a giant cross, alongside which hung a dove in flight. Both the cross and the dove were solid gold.

Sheer wonderment filled their faces. They were mesmerized by the spectacle before them.

"We did it! We found La Dura! Flynn, do you realize, I'm the richest woman in the entire world?"

Flynn was weary. The cold and rain-soaked clothes chilled his body. He was tired and impatient to be gone. His voice rang hard. "Yes, Maria Ropero, you're the richest woman in the entire world, but the riches will do you no good unless we ride out of here tomorrow. We will have what is left of our supplies for dinner. In the morning, we'll load the mules and horses with gold and we'll be on our way to the border."

Maria started to protest, but Flynn raised his hand and stopped her. "Really, Maria, we have no choice. If we don't make a run for the border, our bones will be rotting in some remote canyon like so many before us. We *have* to go."

Sheets of cold rain lashed through the canyon and the night was pitch black. They had changed into dry clothes and sought shelter inside the one room of the cabin that was not destroyed. They ate the last of their supplies by the light of one of the torches and started to put out their bedrolls when Maria put her hand on Flynn's arm.

"I want to apologize for the other night. I didn't mean what I said about not loving you or that you weren't as much a man as my father. I was frustrated and angry, and just trying to be hateful. I do love you and I want to share everything with you. Will you forgive me?"

Flynn looked at her standing there is the torch-light. Outside, the howling wind and slashing rain sealed them in this remote little corner of the world. Her hair that had been drenched earlier was now dry and curly. She looked like a little girl with a beautiful smile and warm red lips.

"You know I forgive you. The things you said hurt, but I know how much this search has meant to you, how at times you've just not been the woman that I first fell in love with."

She slipped into his arms. "Let's forget the past few days. I promise, it will never happen again. I do love you and I want us to be together, always."

Her lips found his and their bodies pressed tightly together. She broke away and went toward her sleeping bag. Quick fingers found the buttons of her shirt and she tossed it into the corner and stood still and tall with her beautiful, hard breasts covered only by the fading torchlight.

"Why don't you put out the torch and come and join me for our last night at La Dura?"

Flynn needed no prodding. He put the torch out and the cabin plunged into darkness. In seconds, her bare shoulders were in his strong hands and the two lovers touched, explored, and at last came together with soft sounds and moans as the timbers of the old cabin creaked and groaned.

Outside, the wind and the rain played a lonely rhapsody for the lovers.

CHAPTER THIRTY-THREE

RAIN CONTINUED TO POUR FROM THE LEADEN SKIES as the thunderheads rode the crest of the Sierra Madre. The creek became a wild, surging stream and the arroyos were overflowing. The animals had been moved to the top of the steps that lead to the treasure house.

They worked by the light of the ancient tapers to conserve what little life was left in their torches as, with aching legs, they carried bars of gold from the levels below.

Wrapped in canvas, the gold had been carefully tied onto the mules. Flynn secured the last sack of gold coins on the horses. "That's it. Let's get out of here and try to make the best time possible before the day is over." He started to mount.

Maria, the rain pouring from the brim of her *tejano*, flashed her most provocative smile. "Honey, I know you're anxious to leave, but before we go, can we look at the treasure house just once more? I want to remember it for always."

Reluctantly, he agreed. "Okay, let's take one more look."

Flynn leaned against the open wood door while

Maria lit the candles that had remained on the altar since the 16th century, and then relit the tapers left behind by the *padres*. Their mixture of fire, smoke and incense gave an eerie feeling of mystical ancient rites. After the last taper was lit, the treasure house gleamed.

Maria snuggled close. "This is the way it must have looked when the *padres* ruled this part of the world. I will never, never forget this moment."

From behind them came the sound of a familiar voice. "I'm very sure you never will!"

CHAPTER THIRTY-FOUR

THEY SPUN AROUND AND FLYNN'S HAND STARTED FOR his gun, then froze. Standing in the doorway to the treasure house was Cory. He was stripped to the waist and the black hair that covered his powerful body glistened with rain water. His jeans were low on his hips and a red rag was tied around his forehead. He was carrying a backpack with a CAR-15 slung over one shoulder while his heavy leather gun belt held the big Magnum; his feet were encased in muddy black boots.

Beside him stood a snarling Timer, water dripping from his Stetson and running down his stringy blond hair. Behind them were two *gringos*, dirty and foul, each with a rifle pointed at Maria and Flynn.

Cory laughed at their surprise.

"Well, Ms. Maria, may I say that your map was very accurate? I'm so glad we arrived before you left. I found two friends and met up with Timer. And here we are. All the family together again. Flynn, it was nice of you to load the gold for us. Now, all we have to do is load our own mules and then we're off to the border."

Flynn realized that the game was over. "Look

Cory, I don't care about myself, but we're out of supplies. Even if Maria leaves right now, she'll be pressing her luck to make it back safely. Let her go."

Cory and Timer burst out with blood-chilling laughter and the *gringos* behind them joined in.

Then Timer, still snarling, stepped forward. "Flynn, what a short memory you have. I was about to enjoy Maria's charms when the late Mr. Poet got into the act. Oh yes, it is the *late* Mr. Poet. You see, Cory took good care of him with his piano wire."

Flynn's eyes narrowed and Maria turned pale at the news.

Cory vigorously nodded his head. "That's true Flynn. That son-of-a-bitch was nothing but a weakling, so I took care of his needs. As if having to travel with him wasn't bad enough, you and your Spic friend cost me that pretty little piece at the cantina, so I'm going to give Miss Maria some pain before we depart, and if our pals here are good boys, they can join me in the fun."

Timer couldn't wait. "Just a second, Cory. Before you drive Maria out of her mind, I'm going to give Flynn the beating of his life."

Maria threw herself in front of Flynn. "No, please, I'm begging you. Do anything you want with me, but leave him alone. It was my fault he drove you out of the camp."

Timer exploded, his lips covered with spittle and his eyes glazed over. "Shut up, woman! You're going to be whipped and tortured, but first I want him! Ringo, hold the woman!"

The largest *gringo* seized Maria, who started struggling, as Timer, Cory, and the remaining *gringo* moved toward Flynn. As they circled around, Flynn's hand reached for the butt of his gun. Cory feinted, moving in and Timer knocked the big Colt from Flynn's hand just as it cleared leather.

For a while, it seemed that in the end Cory, Timer, and the *gringo* would have to rely on their guns if they were to win the fight. Flynn, well-grounded in martial arts from his years as a member of the elite Army Rangers, more than held his own. A slash from the side of a hardened hand left a howling Cory with a broken nose.

Although his opponents had him surrounded, Flynn was able to keep moving and confronting them so that they were unable to gain an advantage. The one *gringo* made the mistake of coming too close and a well-placed kick resulted in a couple of broken ribs that made breathing a difficult task.

Finally, Timer ripped Maria from the hands of the *gringo* guarding her and, using her as a shield, drew his gun and moved in on Flynn. For a split second he diverted Flynn's attention. At that moment Cory smashed the back of Flynn's head with a rifle butt.

Flynn sank to his knees and Cory drove his boot into the side of his neck. As Flynn fell face down, Timer threw the fighting Maria back to the *gringo* guard. He then delivered a killing kick to Flynn's head, just missing his temple.

Grabbing dazed Flynn's arms, the *gringo* with the broken ribs pinned them behind him while Cory and Timer drove their fists into his face and body. Timer jerked a hard knee again and again into Flynn's crotch. Finally, they dropped him to the floor of the treasure house. After what seemed an eternity, they tired of beating and kicking his unconscious form.

Cory gingerly probed his shattered nose.

Timer eyed him with disgust. "Just hold it, tough guy."

Producing a role of tape from Cory's backpack, Timer roughly explored his battered, swollen nose, then gave it a hard jerk that made Cory howl. He then slapped tape over the bridge and pulled it tight. Taking a knife from his pocket, he cut off the loose ends.

Tears ran from Cory's eyes and the fingers of his right hand danced in the air, over the butt of his Magnum, but no matter how bad the pain was, he had enough sense not to draw.

Timer grabbed the *gringo*, who was gasping and sucking with every effort to breathe because of the searing pain from his broken ribs. Timer went into action again with the role of tape. Ripping off the man's shirt, he wound the tape tight around the hairy chest and sweat-covered back while the *gringo* moaned in agony.

After cutting the ends of the tape, Timer slammed the flat of his hand into the *gringo's* back, almost causing him to faint.

"There you are, Steed, all fixed up. Now, get your ass moving and begin loading the gold. I don't intend to hang around here forever. Let's do it!"

Cory stopped the flow of tears and turned his red-rimmed eyes toward Maria, who was still under the control of Ringo.

"Now, my little woman, are you ready to give Cory satisfaction?"

Maria tried to jerk away. "You're nothing but a filthy animal!" She spat in his face and Cory reacted like a streak of lightning.

His ham-like right fist caught her cheek and a portion of her left eye. The blow tore her from Ringo's grasp and she went down. She attempted to stand and smash Cory in his crotch, but his massive right hand caught her again on the cheek and knocked her out.

"You little bitch. I'm going to teach you." His left hand snaked down and grabbed her hair, and then jerked her to her feet. "Throw some water on this bitch. I'm going to teach her a thing or two."

Ringo took a full canteen from his belt and threw the contents into Maria's face. Coughing and sputtering, she came to. Although very groggy, she tried to free her hair from Cory's steely grip.

"Don't you try and get away from me, you little slut. You're going to do exactly as I say."

With a powerful jerk, his right hand ripped her shirt open to the waist, exposing her lush breasts. Between the rounded white mounds sporting coral tips was the Medallion of La Dura.

Cory couldn't believe his eyes. "Timer, look what I found!"

Maria's breasts were rising and falling with anxious breaths as Timer came close and gave a low whistle.

"I thought it was all just a story, not a word of truth in it, but there it is!" He reached forward and ripped off the chain.

Cory caught his arm. "Let me see it."

Timer shook him off as he shoved the Medallion into the breast pocket of his dirty, blood-spattered shirt.

"Later. You don't need to see it now. Why don't you get busy with that little piece you want to work over?"

Cory's face was a mask of hate, but he feared crossing Timer. He turned back to Maria, his black eyes smoldering. "Ringo, Steed, spread her over that rack near the altar. I'm going to give her the taste of my belt, and then I'm going to fix her so no man will ever want her."

The two *gringos* carried a struggling Maria to the far corner of the treasure house. Her shirt was ripped from her arms and she was spread face down over a stack of gold bars. Cory's laughter reverberated around the room as he stripped Maria of her boots. He yanked her jeans down over her rounded hips and long, strong legs. He tore away the silk panties, leaving her firm, smooth buttocks naked. Cory shrugged out of his backpack and laid his Magnum by the altar.

Timer, who was watching the action, noticed that Flynn was starting to show signs of regaining consciousness. He leaned down and whispered in his ear. "You're going to hear your woman scream. Cory's going to whip her nice white body, then use his pliers and a razor. She'll scream a lot. You just listen."

Steed and Ringo stretched the now unresisting Maria's arms as far as possible over the rack of gold and, in doing so ,raised her buttocks in a direct line with the gun belt Cory was snapping behind her.

"Cory, she's not going to give you any trouble and I need Ringo and Steed to get the gold loaded."

They dropped her arms and scurried away before Cory could reply. They went to the far end of the treasure house where they started bringing gold bars to the surface at a dead run.

Hatred for Timer's orders intensified Cory's expression. Watching the two *gringos* snap to Timer's commands was like having salt rubbed in an open wound.

He mumbled to himself, "That son of a bitch. Sooner or later, I'm going to kill him and then the treasure will be all mine."

He turned his attention to the lushness and soft

curves spread out before him. Bringing his belt high, he slashed it across the white body.

It dug into the soft flesh above Maria's left hip, over her back, and across her shoulder. As the leather brought a fiery streak of pain, she grabbed the belt and like a wounded wildcat came flying off the rack of gold.

She caught Cory by surprise and was able to rip the belt from his fingers. Using the solid silver belt buckle in the forward position, she flailed his ape like body with all her strength. The buckle brought blood as it tore flesh from the hairy mat above his navel.

His screams of pain filled the treasure house as the buckle found his broken nose and, despite the protective tape, mashed it flat on his face.

Whirling the belt around her head, the buckle found his kidneys, sending white-hot fingers of pain through his body. As he tried to evade its lashing, it almost tore his right nipple off. Mingling with his screams was the laughter and taunts from Timer, Ringo and Steed, as the trio watched from the treasure house entrance.

With a scream of rage and fury, Cory moved forward just as the buckle destroyed his front teeth, exposing nerves.

But the tide had turned. It seemed that pain was unable to stop him. Although it tore his flesh, he grabbed the buckle and jerked the belt, but Maria hung on. Slowly, he pulled her toward him. He gave the belt a little slack, as if loosening his grip, then jerked forward. His right hand left the belt and his fist buried itself up to the wrist as he jammed it into Maria's stomach.

Her mouth opened as air gushed out of her lungs and pain filled her body. A powerful left hook caught her under her right breast. A right jab caught her just above the line of her pubic hair and a left one hammered high on her jaw, snapping her head, her vision a spinning kaleidoscope. She lost her grip on the belt and reality as chopping rights and lefts sent her head rocking one way, then the other.

Cory snapped his meaty left fist deep into her belly and as she fell forward, a right uppercut hit her jaw like an anvil, sending her sprawling unconscious to the hard-packed dirt floor.

Trying to breathe through his broken nose, Cory stood above her naked form with his mouth open, gasping for breath. Blood flowed freely from his smashed nose, torn belly and nipple, creating small rivers in the thick hair that covered his body.

He raised his eyes to see Steed watching him from across the room.

"What do you think you're looking at you son-of-a bitch? Get me some water. I'm going to bring this hellcat around and then I'm going to carve her up. Move it! And get me some water!"

Steed took off running as Cory bent over slowly and picked up Maria and carried her to the base of the altar. Her face and body were covered with areas where black and purple bruises were forming and angry red welts gave evidence of where the leather belt had taken its toll. Despite the pain throbbing in his nose and broken teeth, he felt the hot flame of lust wash through his body.

With a burst of energy, he removed his remaining clothes and stood naked looking at her limp, beaten body. He moved to a rack of gold and sat down. His greasy face sported a coarse six-day black beard.

The blood around his smashed nose was starting to clot except for a thin trickle that dripped off the right side of his chin. He looked like a big wounded ape. Where his right nipple was torn, the blood had clotted, just as it had above his navel where the belt buckle had torn away a patch of flesh. He grinned with broken teeth as he looked at Maria's battered yet lush body.

He was aroused as he spoke to her unconscious form. "All your education and fancy airs mean nothing now woman; it's just you and me."

Steed's arrival with two canteens of water shook him out of his reverie. Jerking the water away, he bellowed, "Get the hell out of here before I kill you. I'll teach you to laugh at me. I'm going to destroy this woman now, but I'll take care of you later."

Steed beat a hasty retreat, passing the twitching body of Flynn, who was trying to fight his way back to consciousness.

Kneeling by Maria's inert form, Cory talked as he slowly poured the contents of the first canteen over her naked body. "I want you to know and feel what I'm going to do to you. You won't believe that a human can stand such pain ... and live."

A draft of cold air made his sweaty body shudder. It was silent in the treasure house and he jerked up his shaggy head; his wild eyes swept the room. His instincts told him that something was wrong, but his lust for the woman overrode all else.

He went to his backpack and removed a straight razor and long-handled steel pliers. With a growl emanating from deep within his throat, he turned back to Maria.

He straddled her. Laying his tools by her side, he kneaded her full breasts with his huge hands, and then poured the remaining water in the first canteen over her face and body.

She stirred. Cory grabbed her hair and raised her head and forced water between her parted lips. She choked, shaking her head, trying to inch away. He took the cap from the second canteen and forced more water into her mouth. She choked again, then her eyes opened and she lay back, exhausted.

Cory was drooling as he eyed the beautiful body beneath him. "I've waited a long time for this. I'm going to slice your breasts and your belly, and then I'm going to use pliers between your legs and when I'm finished, no man in the world will want your mangled body."

He paused, as if to burn this moment into his brain forever, then reached for the razor and shook the bright silver blade free of its sheath.

Maria only partially heard what Cory had been saying. She had been turning her head right, then left, as if to pick up on an unheard wavelength, but there was nothing to hear. All was deathly quiet and still. She looked at Cory's bloody features and the slack mouth covered with drool. "You stupid animal. Don't you realize Timer and your friends have taken the gold and left you behind?"

Only then was Cory actually aware of the dead silence. The razor fell to the floor. Like a wounded lion, he got off Maria's body, grabbed his Magnum, and raced up the slippery steps from level to level until, at last, he reached the iron door ... where he was greeted by the bodies of Ringo and Steed. Both had steel-tipped arrows buried in their backs.

Cory raised his eyes and, through the rain, saw a grinning Timer, whose finger flicked the trigger of the silent, deadly crossbow.

Cory charged forward and started to bring up the Magnum to fire when a steel arrow tore into his throat. He dropped the weapon and both hands flew to the arrow's shaft in a vain attempt to pull the barbed arrowhead out.

His rain-whipped naked body did a twisting

dance of death. Under the red rag, his eyes blazed with unholy light as blood bubbled from his mouth and flowed downward into the matted hair of his chest and belly.

He forced his body toward Timer. His blood mixed and spattered in the cold sheets of rain pouring from the heavens. The whistling of air through his mashed nose was the only sound to be heard.

In slow motion, Cory sank to the ground, but before he was embraced by the blackness of eternity, his dying eyes watched his blood mix with the rain as it flowed over a nine-pound gold bar that one of the *gringos* had dropped when Timer killed him.

His body twisted. He flopped onto his back, bucking his hips, as if making love to the angel of death. At last he was still, his open eyes staring into blackness as the rain beat his face and the wind whispered, "La Dura."

CHAPTER THIRTY-FIVE

TIMER RELOADED HIS CROSSBOW AND MOVED DOWN the stone steps into the treasure house. Maria was dressed, her torn shirt tied together. She had found Cory's canteen and was giving Flynn a drink. He was attempting to stand when, all of a sudden, he pushed her away.

Timer was in the doorway. His lips were pulled back in a snarl, the flickering candles and tapers making strange patterns on his pockmarked face.

He broke into insane laughter. "Oh, my. Still alive and trying to play the white knight, eh, Flynn? You don't know when it's all over do you? Cory and the *gringos* are dead, and I'm the richest man in the world."

"Timer, you're insane."

"No, Flynn, you're the one who's crazy. You knew long ago that you should get out of Mexico. Your problem was that you couldn't leave this woman. Now, neither one of you will leave. I've always wanted to kill you, and now's the time."

Flynn, used his last bit of strength and dove forward in desperation. Maria also threw herself at

Timer, hoping to take his legs out from under him. Both missed.

Timer's arrow caught Flynn low on the left side and he crashed to the floor. He kicked Maria away, and she rolled up into a ball of pain.

Watching them in their agony, Timer was racked by hysterical laughter. He fell to his knees beside a rack of gold, and slobbered and kissed the gold bars, murmuring that he was the richest man in the entire world. Sanity had left him.

Maria had the look of a wild animal. She pushed herself to her knees, then to her feet. Straining, she grabbed a gold bar, lifted it, and brought it crashing down, just as Timer looked up.

At the last second, he leapt out of the way. Cursing, he kicked Maria to the floor, then grabbed her hair and pulled her to her knees. Reaching into his waistband, he pulled out Flynn's Colt and placed it between her eyes. His finger started to tighten on the trigger, but then slowly he released the tension.

He threw Maria from him and she landed next to Flynn, who was trying to pull himself up to a sitting position.

"You want each other so bad, you can spend eternity together—you and the treasure." He burst into insane laughter.

As if on cue, the laughter stopped. He looked at Maria as if he had never seen her before. In a whisper, he uttered words from his sick mind. "I had planned to take you, Ms. Maria, but you have been badly soiled. You are used goods."

Reaching into his breast pocket, Timer extracted the Medallion. He noticed some spots of blood on its otherwise shining surface. This produced another burst of insane laughter.

When that stopped, he spoke to the Medallion in the voice of a conspirator. "I'm so sorry. Cory never was neat with his blood. He thought he could pull that arrow out of his neck. Poor, hairy Cory, what a sight he was."

Again, peals of laughter echoed over the stacks of gold and the flickering candles. "Now, *I* have La Dura! The treasure is *mine!*" With the Medallion dangling from his left hand and the Colt clutched in his right, he backed out, toward the entrance of the treasure house.

From deep within the earth came an ominous sound. Timer cocked his head and listened as the rumbling of the earth became louder and the walls of the treasure house started to shake.

At first, he was not certain what he was hearing. The dirt above fell in a fine, steady mist, and the ancient wooden beams groaned like a chorus of lost souls. Reaching for the closed door, Timer convulsed into another burst of insane laughter, then froze in his tracks.

Coming down, through the dust-laden air from the timbers above, its forked tongue darting in and out quickly and its tiny eyes gleaming like the black coals of Hell was a giant rattlesnake.

Timer brought up the Colt to fire at the same instant the aged timbers above gave way and a section of the roof caved in. A splintered piece of beam knocked the Colt out of his hand, sending it spinning along the floor.

He reached for the gun in his holster, but part of another falling beam pinned down his gun hand and the massive chunks of falling earth buried him from the neck down, leaving only his head and left arm free. In his left hand hung the Medallion of La Dura.

He was raving; an insane litany of sounds fled his froth-covered lips as the snake, with tongue flicking

and eyes locked on his, came closer toward his exposed face.

In a final effort to escape the fate that had been dealt
him, Timer flung the Medallion at the approaching
rattler. The Medallion missed. It hit a falling piece of
timber and spun into the treasure house, onto the
hard-packed floor. Timer screamed as the rattler
struck and buried its fangs in his face. As the agony
of death racked his body, the elements broke forth in
all their fury.

More timbers, dirt and rocks fell, and then Timer
and the rattler disappeared from sight.

CHAPTER THIRTY-SIX

Maria was on her knees, crying. Flat on the cool dirt floor, Flynn was trying to say something. His right hand was clawing forward, trying to reach the Medallion of La Dura.

From where his face was pressed to the floor, he could see that when Timer threw the Medallion, it hit something that caused a secret spring to activate and it had opened like a locket. Inside, he could see a scrap of parchment.

As he clawed the floor, his fingers made contact with the butt of the CAR-15 that Cory had thrown off. Using the carbine as an anchor, he dragged himself toward the Medallion.

At last, his fingers covered the distance to where it had landed. He made contact with the chain and pulled the Medallion toward him. Once in his hand, he rolled onto his side and called in a weak voice that could hardly be heard over the rumbling of the earth. "Maria! Maria, come here!"

Maria came to his side and knelt beside him.

Flynn indicated the scrap of paper that was visible inside the Medallion. "Very gently, take out the paper and let me see it."

Maria's fingers worked carefully at picking out the little piece of parchment that had been encased for centuries. Finally, she worked it free and gently unfolded it before passing it to Flynn.

The tapers had died. Only the two candles on the altar had not been extinguished. Maria seized one and brought it to Flynn.

He had pushed himself into a seated position against the wall. The arrow was still embedded low on his left side. His voice was strained. "This is a map of this room. There's a secret exit that will take you outside."

"You mean it will take *us* outside."

Flynn was having trouble breathing. "In a minute or two, this light will be gone. The candle on the altar has maybe three minutes left at most. Once the light is finished, we'll be entombed for all eternity.:

Their eyes locked.

"Maria, for a little while I had your love and, for me, that was worth a lifetime. You're the most wonderful thing that ever happened to me."

Tears rolled down Maria's face. "Flynn, I love you. I love you more than all the treasure in the world. I love you more than anything and I want us to leave together and go back home. Rich or poor, we'll have a life together. Don't you see it's the two of us?"

The candle she was holding flickered wildly.

"Maria, if nothing else, you are a survivor. You've had to be. Look, you have to escape for our love to have meant anything. Please, just do what I tell you."

An ominous rumble loosened more dirt as the beams groaned and twisted.

"Flynn, I won't leave without you, ne*ver*!"

Flynn knew he must play the game the only way possible. "Okay, honey, we'll go together. Help me slide over to the other wall where I can get more light on this paper and you do what it says and we'll both be free."

She helped him slide across the dirt floor to where he had enough light to read by. Suddenly, everything was nearly black as the candle almost died. It sputtered, but then took hold again; the time, however, could now be measured in seconds.

"Go to the altar. Reach up and steady the cross."

Maria scrambled to the altar where everything was covered with dirt. She pulled herself up onto the altar so that she could reach the bottom of the huge cross that was swinging from the tremors of the earth.

"Now, step in between the cross and the dove."

Fighting the falling debris and struggling to stand on the dirt-slick area, Maria got into position.

Flynn pushed himself as far up the wall as he could. He reached down to the spot where the arrow was embedded and when he drew his hand back, there was only a small amount of blood.

"Maria, with all your strength, push the cross toward me, then pull down on the dove of La Dura."

Maria used every ounce of her strength, but nothing happened. Flynn's candle died and the light on the altar was sputtering weakly, ready to plunge the treasure house into eternal darkness.

Flynn yelled, "Harder, Maria, pull harder!"

Sweat poured down her dirt-streaked face. Her body strained with the effort, then the altar started to swing. Untouched for centuries, it was turning on its incredibly engineered axis. The trigger had been sprung for the secret exit from La Dura.

The earth cracked above and dirt and rocks poured into the treasure house. Maria screamed.

The walls were buckling and then, as in slow-motion, they came crashing down. For an instant, she saw Flynn ... and then he was gone, hidden by tons of dirt and rocks that had tumbled from above. The racks of gold and silver, the sacks of gold coins vanished as the earth took its vengeance.

Dirt, rocks, and timbers rained down around Maria. The sheer force of the elements threw her on top of the altar, and then she was thrown head over heels in a hailstorm of dirt. She lost consciousness, and slipped down ... down into a dark, endless tunnel.

The candle trembled, flickered, and was gone. What was left of the treasure house was in total darkness. Cracked and splintered timbers, rocks and earth fell but Maria knew nothing during the final seconds of the death throes of the place called La Dura.

CHAPTER THIRTY-SEVEN

From somewhere, a slim shaft of light gleamed, casting a diffused glow on the ruins. The racks of gold and silver, the sacks of coins had vanished, buried under tons of earth. Beneath a broken beam, a rattler slithered through the rubble.

Face down in the dirt, Maria was more dead than alive. At last, she moved her arms, and her fingers closed around the Medallion. Even in her stunned state she seemed to know what it was and pulled it to her.

Ever so slowly, she moved her legs and in stages lifted her head. Her voice was a whisper. "Flynn?"

There was no sound.

"Flynn?"

The silence of the tomb was her answer. She dug her fingers into the wall of dirt and rocks

And, in agony, pulled herself to her feet. She screamed. "Flynn! Flynn!"

Her energy was drained. Slowly, she sank to the floor; violent sobs shook her body. She was a small bundle of dirty rags that whispered softly, "Oh, my God, Flynn. I love you. I love you."

It was so still in this place that the sound of her

sobs carried upward and over piles of earth and rock, and through the ever-swirling dust.

A crack of light seeped down to where Flynn lay flat against the hard-packed earth. His face was peaceful, as if asleep. From somewhere, water licked his boots and the size and force of the water seemed to increase as minutes ticked by.

From afar, like an echo in the wind, was the sound of Maria's voice. "Flynn, Flynn, I love you."

The words bounced around the rocks and timbers. Bit by bit, Flynn's right hand slid forward to touch the wall of earth and stone as he whispered, *"Vaya con dios, mi nivio, me olvides, yo oro."*

CHAPTER THIRTY-EIGHT

Hours passed as Maria drifted in and out of consciousness. Eventually, a faint gleam of light caught her eye. It seemed very, very far away. The fragmented rays showed her something that looked different from the rocks and stones that had come from above and she crawled toward it.

Her fingers touched a webbed strap and she realized that this was Cory's backpack. With the strap wrapped around one arm and the Medallion clutched in the other hand, she started crawling toward the faraway light source.

The going was rough. She snapped what was left of her fingernails, and her fingertips were bloodied from the sharp rocks and pieces of timbers. The closer she came to the light, a roaring sound became louder and louder.

Crawling around a pile of rocks, she was almost blinded by the light and the roar became ear splitting loud. Before her was an opening, maybe eight feet high and four feet wide. Through a diffused veil, the sun was shining in a cloudless sea of blue. She crawled through the remaining rocks and came face to face with a roaring waterfall.

Painfully, she managed to get to her feet. The water raged over her head, plunging into a swirling, rushing river sixty feet below. Could this be what she was saved for, to die on a ledge overlooking freedom?

Any decisions could be postponed for the moment. Sitting with her back to the rocks, she opened Cory's backpack and found several cans of fruit cocktail. She tore open the self-opening cans, drank the juice, and pried out peaches and pears with her fingers, stuffing her mouth until it could hold no more. She found a sack of hard biscuits and a package of dried jerky. Discovering a handheld can opener and a can of baked beans was a bonus. Lying on her stomach, she slid out far enough so that she could fill Cory's tin mug with water from the falls. Never had anything tasted so good.

Returning to the pack, she found her father's maps, a couple pairs of socks, a hunting knife in a leather scabbard, three more cans of fruit, and another pack of jerky. Going back to where the waterfall plunged to the river, she studied the long drop to the rapids below.

She realized there was no other way out. Unless she took her chances diving through the waterfall into the swirling waters, she would die at La Dura.

Hastily removing her dirt-encrusted boots, she threw her soiled, worn socks away. The boots, clean socks, maps, cans of food and the supply of jerky were stuffed into the backpack and the straps adjusted so they fit tightly. After securing the scabbard with the hunting knife to her belt, Maria tucked in her torn shirt.

Lastly, into her shirt pocket went the Medallion of La Dura, broken chain and all. She buttoned it tight, took a deep calming breath, and stepped to the ledge.

With all the strength available in her legs, she dove into the waterfall.

CHAPTER THIRTY-NINE

Spinning like a top, she fell until she vanished into the swirling whirlpool below. Several seconds later, she shot to the surface and struggled to break free of the whirlpool's powerful embrace. The backpack was dragging her under.

After she had plunged down twice, she realized the backpack had to go. Under water, she fought her way out of the tight straps and shot back to the surface—and, finally, broke free of the raging current. Swimming to the grassy side of the stream, Maria pulled out her exhausted self and collapsed.

Time seemed to stand still but, eventually, things came into slow focus: the cascading waterfall and the rushing river, the sun in the bright blue sky shining on the peaks of the Sierra Madre. Downstream, she saw the backpack lodged against some rocks. This would be a welcome break … if her boots were still intact. Trying to get out of Mexico on bare feet was not something she wanted to attempt.

She waded into the stream and recovered the backpack. The maps, jerky and clean socks were gone; two of the three cans of fruit remained jammed in the bottom, and the boots were wet but wearable.

The next three hours she rested by the side of the stream while her boots dried in the sun. She was tempted to eat the canned fruit, but put them in her pockets instead.

Unable to wait any longer, Maria jammed her bare feet into the partially dried boots and started the long winding climb back up the mountain, to the entrance of the treasure house of La Dura.

That night, she slept under some brush halfway on the mountain. Dinner consisted of one can of fruit.

The sun was setting the following day when she reached the site of the *mesa* and the old

line cabin. Crossing the stream, she climbed to the entrance of the treasure house—and stopped dead in her tracks, unable to believe what she saw. The horses and mules were gone.

In front of the great iron door lay the bodies of Ringo and Steed, which had begun to decompose in the heat. Bile rose in her throat as she was forced to step over Cory's naked corpse. Predators had ripped away hunks of flesh, leaving ugly gaping wounds. Ants were having their fill, running in and out of the matted hair and the sightless eyes.

The great iron door was ajar but, behind it, the tunnel was sealed by tons of rocks and dirt. Where the horses and mules had been tied, only parts of broken halters remained. She slumped to the ground as tears filled her eyes. She was weary and hope was lean. Her cheeks were bruised and cut, her hair tangled, and a thick scab had formed on her lip where Cory had hit her.

The putrid smell of the bodies drove her to her feet and she spoke to the wind, as if in a trance. "I am Maria Ropero, owner of La Dura. I am the richest woman in the world."

Strange laughter sounded in her throat and then the laughter evolved into tears. Wiping her eyes with the back of a scratched and torn hand, she again stepped over Cory's corpse and began down the *mesa*. Reaching the creek, she knelt and washed her face in the clear, cold water; using both hands, she cupped enough of the sparkling liquid to satisfy her raging thirst.

Crossing the creek, she walked to the old line cabin and wearily sat under the ramada. She dozed off and awakened to the hoot of an owl and the howl of a lone coyote.

The sun had long gone and a huge silver moon sprinkled its light over the mountains and valley. Leaning back against the cabin, she finished the last can of fruit and threw the empty can toward the creek.

For a long while, she stared at the moon and then spoke to the night. "I'm getting out of Mexico. I'm leaving this Godforsaken place." She slid down and rolled over, her arms supporting her head.

Later that night, she again spoke to the moon. "You know I'm coming back. La Dura belongs to Flynn and me. It is ours ... forever!"

Sleep came as the wind whispered secrets dead in the dust of centuries long gone. Had she awakened, she would have heard the faint chimes of the bells of La Dura.

CHAPTER FORTY

Sleep concluded with the purple and gold hues of dawn. The world was silent. For a moment, Maria thought she was back at her ranch, but then reality set in. Pulling on her boots, she walked to the creek and stretched out on the bank, and drank deeply.

Tearing a strip from the old canvas on the ramada, she tied back her hair and then, with firm and determined steps, headed north.

The first three days, the going was easy. She was coming down through the pines, crossing streambeds, walking between high canyon walls and around thick underbrush. If it were not for having to walk in cumbersome boots, her time would have been better.

For a long while, hunger pains filled her belly, but she was able to put away thoughts of food and concentrate on moving toward the border.

Toward noon of the third day, the whirling blades of a helicopter sounded overhead. Dashing to an open space, she looked up and began to frantically wave. Although the chopper circled, it didn't acknowledge her presence and headed north.

That night, she found water in a small burbling stream and slept between fallen pine boughs.

There was no canteen so, after a long drink from the stream in the morning, she pushed forward. She realized that she had this one last day left in the mountains.

After that, it was all desert.

CHAPTER FORTY-ONE

THE HEAT WAS SIZZLING, CLOSE TO 120 DEGREES. With no hat, Maria's bruised face and lips had started to burn and crack. Her arms were scratched and cut from thorns. Lack of food and water was becoming a serious life-threatening factor and this was only the second full day on the desert. As she traveled, she tripped a few times and everything seemed to go in and out of focus.

In the late afternoon, she again heard the chopper. Squinting skyward, she picked it up as it flew past the sun. Ripping her tattered shirt from her body, she waved feverishly to attract attention.

The copter made a sharp left turn … and then headed north.

Stripped to the waist, she crumbled to the ground and tears filled her red-rimmed, swollen eyes. "Oh God, I can't go much farther in this heat."

Her mind wandered as her eyes tried to focus on the bleak terrain. "Flynn I did my best, I really did. Flynn, I love you, I need you."

Her head bent low as she attempted to collect her thoughts. After a while, Maria realized the sun was burning her naked breasts. Forcing herself to her weary feet, she worked her way into her shirt, and moved slowly and painfully north.

At night, the desert was very cold. Teeth chattering, she curled into a fetal position to stay warm. She had taken off her boots to find raw, red, swollen feet. Her eyes were badly puffed and every inch of skin that had been exposed to the sun had been seared.

There was a suggestion of daylight as she forced her tender feet back into the boots and started walking ... weaving and stumbling. It was still early in the day when she fell and landed on her hands and knees in an arroyo—and came face to face with a coiled rattler. Its tongue flicked as the dark, cold eyes took measure of her.

Ever so slowly, Maria let her right hand slip back to where Cory's hunting knife was fastened to her belt, but then realized there was no way this snake could be stopped with a knife.

Her hand slowly felt along the ground until her fingers encountered a large rock. Maria and the rattler's eyes were locked. The snake struck. She met it in mid-air with the flat side of the rock and, with all her strength, drove the snake's head into the ground.

In a flash, she drew the knife and severed its head. Shudders rippled through her while she watched the body twist and turn as the muscles contracted. With shaking fingers, she lifted the snake's headless body by the tail. Holding it at a distance, she slashed its entire length and then cut out the white meat.

Gagging with every bite, she forced the meat into her mouth. All too soon, it was gone.

Pulling herself upright, she wandered on through the dense desert sand, now and again brushing cacti, whose spines stuck in her arms and legs. Often, she'd fall to the hot, barren ground of the desert and every second the sun was burning ... *always* burning. Her lips had deep, open, crusted cracks and her eyes were burned half-shut.

Out of the blazing stillness of the desert she heard it and then, through the swollen slits her eyes had become, she saw it.

The chopper was circling and circling in long, lazy loops. Surely, the pilot *had* to see her? She tried to scream, but only a croak came out. Then, the chopper was up and away, lost in the heavenly inferno of the sun.

She struggled a few hundred yards more, then fell to the ground.

CHAPTER FORTY-TWO

For a long time, she remained where she had fallen, then slowly she raised her head. Her mind must be playing tricks? No, it was *real*. Someone was racing the engine of a car. It stopped then started, and then there was silence.

With super-human effort, she pushed herself to her feet and moved forward, through the cacti and mesquite, up a small hill.

Working her way through the underbrush, she saw it; in a box canyon below stood an old adobe house. One side of the canyon served as the back wall of the structure. Parked by the side of the house were several horse trailers. An open Jeep was parked in front.

Five saddled horses, complete with bedrolls and rifle scabbards, were tied to the hitching post. There were also eight mules wearing empty pack harness. From inside the house came the sound of male voices.

A spark of hope had never burned brighter. With all the will she could muster, Maria forced herself over the top of the sandy hill. Then slipping, sometimes falling and sliding, she reached the bottom and faced the house.

The broken door swung open and five young *gringos* strolled out. They were armed with handguns. The last man to exit was sniffing a hit of cocaine. He seemed to be the leader.

He looked up to see Maria, who was staggering toward them, trying to scream. "Help me. Won't someone help me?"

The leader broke into laughter. "What is this ugly thing, croaking like a frog? It must be the offspring of a Gila monster."

The others were amused by the sunburned and tattered woman in front of them.

Hearing their laughter, Maria crumbled to the ground and begged,

"Water, please give me some water."

The leader and his men ambled over to where Maria was kneeling. "So, desert hag, you'd like some water?" He pointed to a well behind him. "Why don't you crawl over there and help yourself?"

Maria's swollen eyes darted toward the rim of a well and, from somewhere deep inside, she found the strength to crawl across the yard. The watching men gently punched one another and grinned.

Pulling herself up to the rim, she grabbed the rope and dropped the bucket downward. Grasping the rope, she peered down. The well had been dry for years; only cracked earth remained.

"Empty! Oh ,my God, it's empty."

The men roared with laughter and circled her as she slumped to the side of the well.

The leader pulled her tattered shirt apart, exposing her sun-burned breasts. "Do any of you want to use her? We can strip her and put her on the porch, or we can take her inside."

One man answered with a wry chuckle. "You have to be joking. Who'd want that used-up body? I'd rather mate with an iguana."

The others filled the air with laughter.

The leader took the canteen that was attached to his saddle and took a drink as he looked at Maria. "We have to get moving so that we can make the pick-up and be back here tomorrow afternoon to meet the chopper. The vultures will have reduced what's left of her to bones by the time we return." Closing the canteen, the leader strolled to the horses and mules.

Maria had remained with her head down, but now an emerging insanity prevailed. Her eyes became mere slits on her sunbaked, cut and bruised face. What was once a beautiful woman had been turned into a burned sack of rags by thirst and exposure. She tried to wet her cracked lips with her swollen, parched tongue, but she had no saliva.

When she spoke, everything came out like a croak. "Who do you think you're dealing with?"

The men, who had mounted their horses, stopped to look at her.

Shirt open, sunburned breasts bare, she had forced her body into a standing position using the rim of the well as support. Reaching into her shirt pocket, she drew forth the Medallion of La Dura, still hanging from its broken chain. It was dirty and dusty, but still held a faint sparkle.

"Look, *senores* ... the Medallion of La Dura. I will give you untold wealth. Gold, all the gold in the world, if you will help me. Please ... help me."

The leader convulsed with laughter as he pointed at Maria. "Why don't you help yourself? *You're* the one who needs help."

She was unsteady, ready to fall, but she forced the

words from her cracked and parched mouth. "For God's ... sake ... take my body, my riches, take everything, but just help me."

The leader had grown tired of this sport. "You burned-up hag, nobody wants your body, and as for riches, you never had any."

He indicated the men should ride out. The horses and mules passed Maria.

When the leader came even with her, she staggered forward and grabbed his boot, her battered face looked up at him, and asked for help. "Don't you understand? I am Maria Ropero. I own La Dura. I will give you gold, I will—"

The leader drew his boot out of the stirrup and kicked her free, then put his horse into a run to join the others.

Maria fought to keep her footing. She staggered through the swirling dust, trying to follow. Although it was agony to speak, her attempt at words rang out loud and clear into the hot desert air. "You stupid fool. I am Maria Ropero. I own La Dura ... I am the richest woman in the entire world." Her eyes flashed as if with fever.

The leader and his men stopped at the top of the hill. Nothing moved except the breeze that kicked up small dust devils. He turned to his men. "We are behind schedule. You go ahead and I'll catch up. Go ahead, move!"

The men wheeled their horses and mules and, in a cloud of dust, disappeared over the rim of a sand dune. Slowly, the leader turned his horse. For a long moment, he sat like a statue, then raced to the bottom of the hill, stopping his horse within a foot of where Maria stood.

She looked up and forced the cracked lips to smile, and a tear ran down her bruised cheek. Reaching down with his left hand, the leader took her outstretched right hand and indicated she should step on his boot in the stirrup, and then he pulled her up so that she was eye level.

Her left hand still clung to the Medallion of La Dura with its broken chain. The breeze moved the torn shirt, exposing her sunburned breasts. Her battered face regarded the young, cruel face. Time stretched into eternity.

With a little girl smile, Maria slowly raised her left hand, offering the Medallion of La Dura in exchange for her life.

The leader's eyes never left Maria, but his right hand snaked to his hip and the well-worn butt of his Smith & Wesson. The gun cleared leather as he brought it up in an arc so that the barrel was inches from her face.

Disbelief and terror filled her eyes as he thumbed back the hammer. An ear-splitting roar ripped through the desert air.

CHAPTER FORTY-THREE

ALL WAS SILENT EXCEPT FOR THE CREAKING OF THE broken door on the old house. The air was filled with swirling dust. Maria was face down, crumpled on the desert floor.

Close to her, the leader was trying to stagger to his feet. The front of his shirt was drenched with an ever-widening pool of blood. He wheezed as he muttered, "You bastard, I'll kill you."

The explosion from a rifle drove him into a seated position by the dry well. The gun slipped from his fingers as death glazed his eyes.

Slowly, Maria forced herself up on her hands and knees; then, with one hand, she pushed dirty, matted hair back from her face. She peered toward the sound of the rifle shot … and could not comprehend what she was seeing. "You!"

Stepping from the porch of the house, walking toward her, wearing an expensive western suit with a rifle in his hands, was Randolph Hansen.

"At last, the charade is over. Now you know that I have always held all the cards."

Maria looked as though she had gone crazy. "I don't know what you're saying."

The shadow of a smug smile played around Hansen's lips. "Like everyone else, I was interested in the legend of lost La Dura. I always suspected that your father had left something regarding its whereabouts, but I never guessed the Indio had the information. When I did find out, it was too late to arrange for him to have an accident. I had to go to another plan."

"How did you know I would be here?"

Hansen acted as though he were passing information to a small child. "Once you hired Flynn, I knew he needed men and I saw that he got them. I sent him both Timer and Cory, and he never suspected. Poet was something else. That just happened, but he was no problem.

"When Flynn forced Timer to leave the expedition, he called me from the railroad spur. He knew Cory had stolen your maps. We discussed his return to find La Dura and to get rid of both Cory and Flynn. When he didn't come back in a reasonable time, I started tracking you by helicopter."

Maria was unable to believe what he was saying. "You mean that was *you*? You could have come down and saved me. I might have died."

Hansen's eyes were hard slits and his face was twisted with hate. "Oh, no. I wouldn't let you die, but you had to be punished. I wanted you to suffer. Suffer the way I've suffered when I saw you going out with lesser men than myself, animals like Flynn, pawing and slobbering all over your beautiful body while, all the time, I was being passed over.

"Ah, but you have paid. You failed to recognize my brilliance. It was I who caused your ranch to have losses. It is I who owns the majority of stock in the development company that will now take over your property. It is I who saw that your trusted friend and advisor, Mr. Alvarez, had an unfortunate accident soon after you left with that scum Flynn."

Maria struggled to her feet. "What kind of a monster are you?" She pointed at the dead leader slumped by the well. "Why did you kill him? Certainly not to protect me?"

Hansen moved closer with an unsettling giggle and the tic near his eye was more pronounced.

"He died because he thought he could steal from the cartel where I am a major player, My shipments of cocaine, a little side business nets me millions."

Lust surged through him and he felt a throbbing in his groin as he gazed at Maria's exposed breasts. Another giggle escaped his lips.

She followed his gaze and pulled the tattered remains of her shirt together.

"Enough of this. The chopper returns for me in five hours and I must tidy up." He snatched the Medallion of La Dura from Maria's grasp and examined both sides. "Now I have all the pieces ... the information Timer gave me from your father's maps and the Medallion." Again, a ragged giggle escaped.

"You'll never get away with this. Somehow, I'll get to the border and justice will be—"

Her speech ended abruptly as Hansen gave a jolting slap, knocking her to the ground.

The swirling dust, stirred up by the afternoon breeze, was once again evolving into dust devils.

He came and stood over her. Insanity blazed in his eyes, stark hatred darkened his face, and the tic was uncontrollable. "I *am* justice! I am *your* judge, *your* jury, and I will be *your* executioner." He turned, took five steps, then whirled.

"Maria Ropero, the verdict is *death*! Stand up, you slut. The Roperos are supposed to be so brave. Stand up and die."

The shirt opened as Maria struggled to her feet. For once, her body failed her and she collapsed to the ground, but her eyes never left Hansen. She whispered, "I am not afraid."

Hansen tossed the Medallion of La Dura to one side. He brought the rifle to his shoulder and squinted through the gunsight.

Maria's haunted eyes were calm as his finger squeezed the trigger.

CHAPTER FORTY-FOUR

THE BULLET THAT TORE INTO HANSEN'S BODY SPUN him halfway around. His shot went over Maria's head as he crashed to his knees.

Advancing through the swirling dust was Flynn with Cory's carbine in his hands. He was stripped to the waist, sunburned and dirty. A bandage made from his old blue shirt covered his left side. His face was dark with a growth of beard and he was yelling, "It's over, damn you. It's over!"

Hansen looked as if he had seen a ghost. "It can't be. If Timer and Cory are dead, *you* should be, too!"

Flynn advanced to within ten feet of where Hansen was resting on his knees. "Sometimes, it's better to be lucky. I could have never escaped La Dura, except there was an underground river and after the earthquake, it flowed into the treasure house, literally floating me to an opening in the mountain.

"Once outside, I spotted the chopper, which gave me a fix on the direction Maria had probably headed. I didn't survive the hell of Iraq and Afghanistan to be killed by the likes of you, or lose the woman I love."

The remark about loving Maria lit Hansen's fuse. He struggled to his feet, despite the fact he had already lost a lot of blood. "You scum. Do you really think you're half as smart as I am? Just for one second, did you ever think you could be as brilliant as I am? You're nothing but a fool, a loser. You lost La Dura, and now you've lost her!"

Hansen spun toward Maria and attempted to fire from the hip. Before he could pull the trigger, however, Flynn's shot tore into his groin and staggered him.

Feeling his lifeblood gushing from his body, Hansen tried to bring the rifle to bear on Maria once again, but Flynn's shot tore the weapon from his grasp and slammed him to the ground. A fountain of blood soaked his chest.

Flynn dropped the carbine and went to the leader's horse, where he stripped the canteen from the saddle. Through the swirling dust that broke the sun's rays into a million fragments, he walked to where Maria was sprawled facedown. Rolling her over, he then picked her up and carried her to the shade of the porch.

Gently, he placed her on her back and supported her with one arm. Uncapping the canteen, he let a trickle of water run over her cracked and burned face.

Slowly her lips opened, a little water entered her throat and she swallowed.

He eased her down. Ripping off a piece of his bandage, he wet the cloth and softly washed her face.

At last, her eyelids fluttered open, and she stared with disbelief and wonder as tears cascaded down her cheeks. "I don't believe it. God has given me a miracle. Flynn, I love you ... I love you."

His hand softly touched her lips. "Don't try to

talk. You're safe now and I'm taking you home." Very gently, he placed his lips on hers.

After he bathed her face, from time to time, he gave her small drinks of water. When it was empty, he threw the canteen away, then lifted her in his arms and carried her to the Jeep.

After fastening her safety belt, he slipped behind the wheel, turned the key, and the engine responded. Slowly, they left the house behind.

Maria, struggling in her seat, mumbled through cracked lips, "Please, stop."

He brought the Jeep to a halt.

Maria pointed. "Look, I forgot something."

There, in the dust of the desert, still attached to its broken chain, was the Medallion of La Dura.

Flynn jumped out of the Jeep, picked up the Medallion and handed it to her.

She held it close to her face, as if seeing it for the first time. "The lives this has cost, the agony, the destruction."

Flynn, back at the wheel, nodded, his expression grave. "We know your father lost his life, then Jesus, Poet, Timer, Cory, Alvarez, Hansen, and who knows how many others. This greed for gold has come very close to destroying us."

Maria stared at the Medallion. "From the time I was a little girl, I remember they always said that La Dura was of the buried past, yet it remained the hope of men and women searching today ... and making plans to search tomorrow." She took a one long last look at it and then, with the speed of light, threw it onto the desert.

Turning in her seat, she came into Flynn's arms. "We already have the greatest treasure of all, we have each other."

Softly, they kissed.

Finally, he broke away. "We're going home, Maria, you and me. We're going home."

The Jeep gathered speed, turning away from the hill, heading for the border. It left a thick trail of dust behind it that seemed to hang in infinity until the vehicle was a speck on the horizon, and then faded from sight.

EPILOGUE

The sun was a great ball of fire, sinking in the west. In this lonely place, where only the dead kept watch, the soft breeze played through the mesquite and chaparral.

For a brief moment, the sun sparkled on something. There, in the dust of the desert, awaiting discovery, as it had waited through eons of time, was the Medallion.

From far, far away, thin and eerie, could be heard the faint echo of mission bells and the ghostly wind whispered softly, as it had for centuries.

"Come ... come to La Dura."

Dear reader,

We hope you enjoyed reading *Gold Envy*. Please take a moment to leave a review, even if it's a short one. Your opinion is important to us.

Discover more books by Rena Winters at https://www.nextchapter.pub/authors/rena-winters

Want to know when one of our books is free or discounted? Join the newsletter at http://eepurl.com/bqqB3H

Best regards,

Rena Winters and the Next Chapter Team

ABOUT THE AUTHOR

Multi-talented Rena Winters has enjoyed an outstanding career in the entertainment industry as a writer, talent, producer, production executive and as a major TV and Motion Picture executive.

Her writing ability won the coveted Angel Award for the "outstanding family TV special, "How to Change Your Life" which she co-hosted with Robert Stack. She wrote (and co-produced) the two-hour script for *My Little Corner of the World*, winner of the Freedoms Foundation and American Family Heritage awards.

Feature films include *The Boys Next Door, KGB, the Secret War, Charlie Chan & the Curse of the Dragon Queen, and Avenging Angel.*

Her producing credits include *The Juliet Prowse Spectacular* for 20th Century Fox, *Sinatra—Las Vegas Style* and *Peter Marshall—One More Time*, which produced a bestselling soundtrack album.

As Executive Vice President, she headed the entire USA operation for the international entertainment giant, Sepp-Inter, producers of TV series, TV specials, feature films and all areas of merchandising for their animated entities including *The Smurfs, Flipper, Seabert, The Snorks* and *Foofur* (all Emmy award winners), plus *After School Specials* for CBS-TV.

Author of the bestselling book *Smurfs: The Inside Story of the Little Blue Characters*, it is currently available on Amazon and Kindle, and in all book stores.

Contributing author to an anthology of patriots

and heroes, *I Pledge Allegiance*, sponsored by the Wednesday Warriors Writers group, it is currently on Amazon and Kindle.

The latest book, *Target One*, is a story about how terrorism escalates in America. It is the winner of 2nd Place Best Fiction 2018 by the Public Safety Writers Association.

Rena is a contributing writer to the summerlin-ww.blogspot.com as a member of the Summerlin Writers and Poets Group. She is also a contributing writer to WTTmagazine@gmail.com. She is a former writer/reporter for thenowreport.vegas, an online newspaper.

In addition, Rena has recently completed writing a children's book featuring two rescue cats. She also has a forthcoming cookbook for people who don't have time to cook.

Rena Winters was voted one of the "50 Great Writers You Should Be Reading – 2017 and 2018" by The Authors Show.com.

At the College of Southern Nevada, Rena is an adjunct instructor teaching Creative Writing courses. She makes her home in Las Vegas, Nevada, and works in her spare time as an editor and ghostwriter.

Gold Envy
ISBN: 978-4-86747-971-1
Mass Market

Published by
Next Chapter
1-60-20 Minami-Otsuka
170-0005 Toshima-Ku, Tokyo
+818035793528

30th May 2021